"Friends can get you into the damnedest things! In this case, a dying man changes the main character's life in every way (romance, money and danger) when he makes a request that only a true friend would perform. Charles Hayes...has a way of creating stories that quickly ensnare the reader... I loved this story because of the characters, the plot, and the setting."— *Mark Vogl, author of Southern Fried Ramblings with Grits and All the Fixins, and his column "America Today" at Nolan Chart in Washington, D.C.*

"A leisurely, character-rich novel with a strong Texas flavor, *Briefcase* was one of those one-sitting reads for me. It wasn't that I couldn't put it down. I simply didn't want to. Like going to a party where you actually like most of the people there, you're having fun and you're in no big hurry to go home."— *Tom King, author of Going for the Green.*

"I must say *The Brief Case* is a very intriguing, and suspenseful mystery! It holds a very exciting and interest throughout the whole book. I did not want to stop reading until the end. It was very exciting and kept me on the edge of the seat until the very end!"— *Valory Elliot, author of An Act of Honor and soon to be published An Act of Revenge.*

"Charles Hayes... is a gifted artist, cartoonist, a sculptor in the same league with Frederic Remington and Charles Russell, and a solid, knowledgeable historian. He can now add "novelist" to his amazing list of achievements. *The Briefcase* is a compelling, evocative story, with great characterizations, written in a style that has the reader's complete attention...from the beginning. The very first sentence will capture the reader, creating a desire to read it all; and, having read it all, he will wish for more."— *Lieutenant Colonel Tom C. McKenney, USMC (Ret), award-winning author of "Jack Hinson's One-Man War"*

ALSO BY CHARLES HAYES

*THE GRAY AND THE BLUE—A Comic
Strip History of the Civil War*

Civil War Limericks (Forthcoming)

THE BRIEFCASE
CHARLES HAYES

Moonshine Cove Publishing, LLC
Abbeville, South Carolina U.S.A.

ISBN: 978-1-937327-37-8
Library of Congress Control Number: 2013957222

Book and Cover design by Moonshine Cove; cover photographs public domain images.

ABOUT THE AUTHOR

Charles Hayes earned a bachelor's degree from Rice University in Houston and a Master's degree from the University of Texas in Austin. Both degrees are in physics.

After retiring from Lockheed-Martin in Huntsville, Alabama, where he worked as an analyst of military weapon systems, he moved with his wife Natalie to Tyler, Texas, in 2000.

Hayes is an accomplished sculptor, having won numerous awards in juried art shows, including the Central South Art Exhibition in Nashville. He is still active in art, maintaining an Internet art gallery where he displays the work of many other artists as well as his own.

In addition to mysteries, Hayes writes and delivers talks about the Civil War, and has authored two published books on that subject.

His Web address is: www.b17.com/hayes

His Facebook address is:
www.facebook.com/charles.h.hayes.

To my brother, Thomas Paine Hayes, III

The Briefcase

CHAPTER 1
GOODBYE, PAL

The best friend I ever had pulled the dirtiest trick of my life on me, and he was dead when he did it.

I'm sure he never meant me any harm—just a little inconvenience as owed by one friend to another—when he handed me that manila envelope. It wasn't even sealed; the metal tab clasp was simply bent closed. It had my name on it handwritten in black ink from a felt marker, "Michael Kidd," and under that, "To be opened immediately upon my death." Under that, still with the felt marker, were his signature and the date. The date was that of the very day he gave it to me. That would be a little over a year ago.

It was January, overcast and dreary but not very cold. Through Vince's hospital window I could see the wind gently toying with the limbs of the live oaks growing in the plaza three stories down. The other trees were in their winter nakedness, their skeletal arms unable to grip the mild wind.

"You're kidding," I had said, and tried to give the envelope back to him. He wouldn't take it.

"No, keep it," he said. "I'm serious."

"You aren't going to die for a long time. You've come back from worse shape than this before."

"Let's cut the bullshit," Vince said. He sounded more annoyed than sad, not downcast at all, as if he were talking about a bill that was a little too high but had to be paid anyway. He was partially elevated but not quite sitting up in the hospital bed. A tablet computer lay beside him, displaying a solitaire chess game. He was wearing a moustache of clear plastic tubing. I'd never seen him with a real moustache, and his head, bald from chemotherapy, told me he wasn't likely to grow one soon.

"Vince," I said, "You've been about to die for the past ten years. You've always bounced back when a new treatment was tried. This has been going on ever since they just sewed you up after that first surgery. You've been on the verge of death so many times that it's old stuff."

After his operation years ago, exploratory surgery to see just what that palpable lump in his abdomen was, they took a good look at his internal organs, saw how the cancer had spread, and just sewed him back up without removing anything. I wrote him off as a dead man then. I had learned to associate "inoperable" with "incurable" and imminent death. But in a few months he was back playing softball and managing his small research and development company.

In about a year he started downhill again and became so weak and emaciated I wrote him off again. He talked his doctor into trying some new treatment and made another spectacular recovery. Then the cancer regrouped and made another attack. Again Vince recovered. But each recovery brought him back not quite to his previous peak, and each recurrence reached a new low.

I don't know in how many hospital rooms I had visited him—different hospitals and in different rooms in the same hospital. This room displayed several flower arrangements, including one from me. Vince had many friends and a large family, and his employees liked and respected him. I don't care how many flowers are crammed into it, a hospital room never smells good; but this time, for the first time, Vince's room held the smell of death. No, Vince would not grow a mustache soon. Or ever.

"I've used up my options. There aren't any more treatments."

"Not even experimental ones?"

"None that I can qualify for. When your blood count gets as bad as mine, they won't let you participate in any more trials. So I repeat, let's cut the bullshit. I'm depending on you to open that envelope and do exactly as I say in the note inside. That'll mean you've got to hang around town until I die, because you won't have a lot of time to do what I've set down for you to do."

I only nodded. That was because I could hardly keep the tears out of my eyes as it was. If I tried to say anything I was afraid I would choke up and give the game away. The cancer would win all right, but as much as it had ruined his body, it never laid a glove on Vince himself. The real Vince, the part that transcends the body, the part where character and courage reside, was undiminished.

Over the past years I had driven him several times the two hundred miles from Tyler to Houston and as many times the one hundred miles to Dallas, for treatments. I had never heard him voice resentment at his fate or shed a tear or a groan when I knew he was in extreme pain. The cancer had won all right, but it hadn't humbled Vince. His head was bloody but unbowed. I looked at the scrawny body the cancer had left him with—he was once a fine athlete—and thought I would be proud to be half the man Vince Talbot was at that moment.

So I took the envelope and went home to wait for Vince to die. I figured I would see him a time or two before he cashed in his chips, and maybe I would find a way to say "I love you, Vince" without embarrassing both of us. But it turned out that was the last time I saw him.

It was just a few days later, at eleven o'clock at night that I got the call from Vince's sister Myra. I got out the manila envelope and stared at it for several minutes before I opened it. It's hard to describe what I felt, but somehow I didn't want to know what was inside. It was as if Vince was still alive somehow, and opening the envelope would kill him. I guess it was because this would be the last communication I would have from him, and I didn't want it to end. As long as I didn't look inside, I could postpone the final goodbye.

After awhile, of course, I did open it. Inside were a key, a note, and a copy of Vince's will. I put the will aside as not really being any of my business and unfolded the note. It was handwritten.

To Michael Kidd,

The enclosed key is to my house. Immediately upon my death, go to my house. In my bedroom closet find a locked black valise on the floor in the corner. Remove it, and without opening it or discussing it with anyone, as soon as practicable take it to a secluded area and burn it completely with all its contents.

That, along with his signature, was all there was.

CHAPTER 2
FULL HOUSE

With a population of about one-hundred thousand, Tyler, Texas, is more a small city than a big town. It's full of money and pride with a slightly pretentious veneer of culture. It was made by the oil boom of the 1930s, which turned hard scrabble farmers into rich people overnight and their children into millionaires when they inherited the farms. The children moved into town and built big houses on the little rolling hillsides west of downtown and competed with one another through their gardeners in growing azaleas.

Nowadays the new money was mainly high-tech or medical, and it built mostly south of town in gated neighborhoods fenced with brick and containing golf courses. When Vince's company started raking in the chips, though, he decided he wanted to live among the old money with their huge lots. So he bought an old place, a show piece in the fifties, and remodeled it.

Vince had said to go immediately to his house, but it was midnight by the time I adjusted enough to the fact of his death to function well so I decided to go early the next morning. I didn't fall asleep until almost dawn, so I didn't get up as early as I had planned.

As usual, Buddy was already up and, as usual, he had buttoned his shirt wrong. While I was fixing his shirt I told him about Vince. It's always hard to predict how Buddy will react to important news. Sometimes it has no effect on him while at other times he gets unduly excited. This time his reaction was the same as you would expect from a normal person, he started crying softly, just as I felt like doing.

"Vince is dead," he said, and every once in a while he would stop crying long enough to repeat, "Vince is dead."

I put my arm around his shoulders and we both sat there for a long time, he sobbing while my tears went without vocal accompaniment silently down my cheeks. After awhile he stopped crying.

"Listen, Buddy. I've got to go out. Let's just have some cereal for breakfast and I'll bring back some hamburgers for lunch. Will that be all right?"

"Vince is dead," Buddy said.

"Yes, we'll miss him. He was a good guy."

"His phone number is 903-534-2568."

"That's right, Buddy."

"His cell phone number is 903-985-2569."

"That's right, Buddy."

"His birthday is February 16. How old was he?"

"He was forty-three"

"Then he was born on a Tuesday."

"If you say so, Buddy."

I'd stopped checking Buddy for accuracy years ago. He never missed.

He seemed to be his usual cheerful self by the time we'd finished our Grape Nuts. As usual, I made him promise not to try to cook anything while I was gone. I prefer a gas range, but we had an electric one because you couldn't fill the house with gas by letting something boil over and put out the flame.

I watched while Buddy turned on his computer and went to the Gutenberg Project site. They have thousands of books that you can read online. Unfortunately, they are mostly novels and he prefers non-fiction. What he really enjoys is a text book, high school or college, on just about any subject, and he had a goodly collection of them. But he reads one in only about two hours, and I couldn't afford to keep buying them. Before I discovered Gutenberg, every few days I used to swing over to the Tyler public library and check out some biographies or how-to-do-its for him, but he really liked to possess them. I'd always have to explain why I had to take them back.

His private collection was neatly shelved and he would cycle through them, turning them upside down when he was finished with them. He wouldn't necessarily read them again—he had them memorized—but he would take one off the shelf, flip through a few pages, and just sit and hold it for maybe half an hour. Every ten minutes or so he would open it and turn rapidly to some page that was in his mind and reread that page. When he was finished with it he would replace it on the shelf with the title on the spine lined up with the books on its left and opposite to the ones on its right.

It was another typical winter day in East Texas, overcast but the high was predicted to be in the fifties. It turned out I didn't need Vince's key to get into his house. When I got there at 9 a.m. there was a family reunion in progress.

Vince's note said I should immediately go to his house. I cursed myself for not going at once on receiving word of his death from Myra. Maybe no one would have been in the house then, but I had waited until morning, letting several hours go by, time enough for relatives to come in from out of town and out of state. Of course, Myra could have called them before she called me. For all I knew they could have been there for days waiting for Vince to die.

Now I wondered if I would encounter resistance in removing the briefcase. There was no doubt in my mind that I would leave with it; the question was would I be able to do it without rankling these people? They were, after all, Vince's heirs and they could resent a stranger walking out with what could be a part of his estate.

Myra opened the door for me. It turned out she and her husband were the only persons that I knew in the house. They lived in Dallas, about two hours away, and I had met them when Vince was in Dallas for treatments and a few times at Vince's house. Myra was dressed as if she'd just come from a party. The times I'd seen her before she had also looked as if she had just come from a party. She was wearing a black dress, but a string of pearls kept it from looking like mourning clothes. Raymond, her husband, came up to stand beside her. He was wearing khakis with a striped knit shirt, short sleeves so I assumed he wasn't going out of the house for awhile.

We exchanged condolences and Myra drew me inside and introduced me to her father. The resemblance between Vince and his father was startling. When the old man held my hand and looked into my eyes I saw Vince—not the Vince as I had known him before his sickness but the Vince of his last few months, tall, gaunt and bald. It struck me that old age is also a disease, invariably fatal, a sort of slow motion cancer, with symptoms of progressive weakness, exhaustion, and pain. Maybe someday they'll find a cure for it.

"Vince spoke highly of you," he said.

"He loved you," I told him, and I knew that was true. He looked as if he was going to choke up, so I patted his hand and let Myra lead me to the next relative.

Myra introduced me to the others one or two at a time as "Vince's closest friend, Mike Kidd." I had never laid eyes on any of them, but they all seemed familiar with my name. There were four relatives and their spouses and kids plus a single woman, Vince's younger sister, Vanessa, still in her twenties and a looker. She was the youngest of the family— Vince must have already finished high school when she was born.

Vince's two brothers and their families had driven down from Missouri, all in the same RV. Vanessa was from the same area but had come alone in her own car. The oldest of the siblings, Jacob was tall, like Vince and his father, and soft-spoken. He had the same unruly, straw-colored hair that Vince had before the chemotherapy although Jacob's was beginning to thin. He was friendly enough but I can't say the same for the younger brother, Paul. He was about my age, that is, thirty-six, or maybe a year older, and I soon picked up an air of hostility. Paul was tall like the rest of the Talbot men. He had a couple of inches on me and was about my weight, but not as muscular though he looked as if he could take care of himself. He had the same hair as his brothers, and probably his father until baldness stole it.

Vince and I had spent a lot of time together, but he hadn't talked much about family. Vince liked to talk about ideas, not people, so I knew little about any of his relations. On the other hand, Vince knew all my family—both members, Grandpa and Buddy.

I was standing by Vanessa when Paul gestured for me to accompany him. "Are you as much into games as Vince was?"

We went into Vince's game room and Vanessa tagged along. Vince had collected games. He was more fascinated by them than anyone I had ever known. Pinball machines lined one wall of the huge room, and there was a row of electronic games with laser driven interactive features. A full-size pool table occupied the center of the room.

"No," I said. "But Vince and I did play many a game of scratch or eight ball on this table. Vince usually won. I was never much interested in pinball or these other games."

"Monopoly was one of his favorites back home. I see he has a set here," Vanessa said, pointing at a shelf where Vince had kept his board games. "Did you play that with him?"

"Only once," I said. "There were four of us. He won."

"Only once," Paul said, "Since you were such close friends I would think you played many games with him."

"Vince was too serious about it for me. When the game began to lag I wanted to swap property, or roll dice for it—anything to get some action going. Vince wouldn't do anything to shorten the game unless he could see a real advantage for him in it. It could take all night to play a game of Monopoly the way he played."

"How about poker? Vince loved poker. I bet you played regularly with him, being his best friend and all."

"Sometimes," I said, ignoring what I took to be sarcasm. The octagonal poker table where Vince had hosted weekly games was still set up in the room although it must have been unused for the last several months. "Vince was one of the best poker players I've ever seen. He could have made a good living at it."

"Better at it than you?"

"Absolutely, especially when the stakes were high. Vince had the knack common to all really good poker players of dismissing from his mind the value of the chips. With high stakes I always had trouble not reminding myself that the bet was a month's income.

It's just chips to the professionals, just matchsticks. No matter what the stakes, with Vince it was always just a game and he played all games to win"

"In short, he was better than you at just about everything?" His smile looked to me like a smirk, and I told myself to remember he was Vince's brother.

"There's a ping-pong table top that can be set on top of the pool table," I said. "I could hold my own with Vince on that."

"I should think so, given his physical condition."

I had been trying to like him but it wasn't working. "Of course, I was referring to the time before his decline. As you know, Vince was an extraordinarily intelligent person with considerable athletic ability and a fascination—you could almost say an obsession—with games of all kinds. Naturally he was good at them, and I'm not ashamed to say he could beat me at most of them. As for poker, he was better than I was but I play a pretty good game. My weakness is I tend to call just to see if somebody is bluffing."

Vanessa decided to enter the conversation. "Vince said he met only one person who could beat him at chess. Was that you?"

"We used to play a lot," I said. "He won his share of the games."

"But you won the most, didn't you?"

"Yes."

Vanessa smiled at her brother, and he walked out of the room. I couldn't see much family resemblance in her. She was about medium height whereas the other siblings and Vince's father were tall, and she was darker, her hair almost black and her eyes were large and brown and almost luminous. She probably took after her mother who I knew had died a few years ago, but I couldn't be sure because I'd never seen a picture of her.

"I apologize for Paul's manners," she said. "Sibling rivalry, I guess. They were the two closest in age and he always acted as if he was in competition with Vince. Because Vince could outdo him at everything, he doesn't like to think that anyone was better than Vince at anything. Somehow it annoys him. Vince made him feel second rate. Anyone beating Vince makes him feel third rate."

"There's always somebody better. Vince played a good chess game, I played a better one. We both played much better than the average casual player, but neither of us could have put up a real fight against a professional. Even the local chess club probably has several members that could make me look sick. Paul needs to learn the old cowboy saying, 'There never was a horse that couldn't be rode and there never was a man that couldn't be throwed'."

"Yes, he does." She smiled.

I smiled back. Neither of us seemed to have anything more to say. Some of the houseguests wandered in and out of the game room while we stood there looking at each other. When the silence became awkward I said, "I need your help."

"How?"

"I need to pick up something from Vince's bedroom. He left me a note asking me to. It's something he didn't want anyone to see. I'd hoped to do it without calling attention to it, but with all the people here I don't think it's possible." I had Vince's note with me but I didn't want to show it unless I had to. I didn't think Vince would have wanted me to.

"I'll go with you," Vanessa said. She didn't have the classy look of her older sister, the tall blonde. Myra always wore something stylish and looked like she belonged at a cocktail party. This girl was dressed in jeans, sneakers, and a size XL T-shirt. I guessed that was for comfort during the long drive. I could imagine her in something fashionable giving Myra a run for her money, although she still wouldn't have that patrician look. Pretty rather than beautiful, she struck me as somebody you could have a beer with and relax.

She went with me to the master bedroom and watched me as I opened the closet. The valise was just as Vince had described it, sitting just where he said it would be. I picked it up and walked back over to Vanessa.

"I'm going home now," I said. "I'm the only one in the house that's not related to Vince, and I don't want to intrude any more into family matters."

She nodded and we walked back down the hall to the foyer. We said a few words about the funeral arrangements. I took her hand briefly, smiled and moved toward the front door.

"Where do you think you're going with that briefcase?' Paul called out. He came up to me and reached for the valise. I stepped away from him. This was exactly what I had been trying to avoid but I had given my word to a dying man, my best friend, and I was going to leave with that valise no matter how many relatives tried to stop me.

He took a stand between me and the doorway, and crossed his arms in front of his chest. His face was red, and he was breathing heavily. I could hear more people moving into the foyer. He appeared to be too excited for someone used to fighting, and I didn't want to hurt him, mainly because he was Vince's brother and I liked the rest of the family. But better to go ahead before Jacob and the other men got involved and I wound up hurting people I respected.

I have a knack of tailoring my speech to blend in with whatever group I'm with. I'm an oral chameleon. It's not intentional. I do it without thinking. Put me in an Irish pub and in a little while, damned if I don't develop a brogue. When I'm in a gathering of intellectuals, my grammar and pronunciation just automatically scale up and my accent becomes hard to pin down, American but not regional. But in my fighting mode my language reverts to the pure East Texas dialect I learned growing up on my grandfather's farm.

"You're standin' where I'm fixin' to walk," I said.

There was a change in Paul's eyes. It was the kind of change that happens when you take a stick to poke at what you think is a chicken snake and it suddenly moves into a coil with a spear-shaped head at one end and a rattle at the other. I'll give him credit; he swallowed audibly but he didn't move out of my way. To get out the door I would have to go through him, and I was leaving with the briefcase. And I was leaving now.

CHAPTER 3
BURNING QUESTION

I was afraid the briefcase might fly open if I hit Paul in the head with it, spilling Vince's secrets all over the parquet floor. At the same time I didn't want to set it down. I wasn't going to let it out of my possession even for a moment. So my plan was to kick his shin and ram the corner of the valise into his gut. I hoped that would be enough to clear him out of my path. Out of respect for Vince, I didn't want to do any serious damage to his brother.

"Don't be an ass," Vanessa told her brother. "You know he has a perfect right to remove that briefcase."

"Maybe so, but not until I see what's inside."

"He's got a note from Vince telling him not to open it."

Paul unfolded his arms. "Did you see the note?"

"Yes. He showed it to me." That surprised me.

"Did you read it?"

"Yes." I fell in love with her.

Paul moved aside, and I opened the door. Just before I stepped out I turned and nodded to the group. I climbed into my red Toyota pickup, started it, and headed out. I turned on the radio and pushed buttons to pass over several commercials and political talk shows searching for some soothing country music. I had to settle for a mariachi band. *Thanks, Vince, old pal. Nothing to it. The sheriff will probably be at my house by the time I get there.*

I really didn't think the sheriff would be waiting for me at home, but I headed east out Highway 64 toward Grandpa's farm. I was going to get this business of briefcase burning over with in a hurry. I stopped at a convenience store and bought two pint cans of charcoal starter fluid and a box of matches. After turning onto a county road and following it north for a couple of miles, I turned off at Grandpa's gravel driveway and went over his cattle guard and eventually pulled up at his house.

Grandpa and the house were built in the same year. I guess he was the cause of the house being built, because he came first, in October, eighty-eight years ago. They both are of solid construction, and it's anybody's guess which will last longer.

Grandpa always surprises me by being shorter than I remember him. I guess my mental images are from when I was a kid, shorter than he was; now he's just over five feet and I'm just under six. He has shrunk some, as old people do, but he was short even when I was a kid, short enough for someone to occasionally call him Shorty. He would allow a man to call him that only once. "My name is Tom he would say," making sure he had the fellow's attention. Then he would wag his finger and say, "Don't ever call me Shorty again." Once warned, a repetition of the offense, even if good natured, would trigger an instant fast and powerful punch that would usually be both the start and the finish of a fight.

Grandpa had been an amateur boxer in his youth and more than one trainer had urged him to go professional. He didn't because he valued intelligence and was smart enough to know that he would be progressively less smart after each punch to the head. He had given me my first boxing lessons, and they were sound.

In his prime, Grandpa was the strongest man for his size I ever saw, and he had been quick and graceful in motion. Considering his age, he still was.

When I pulled up to the house he was standing in the yard talking across the corral fence to his favorite riding horse, a big bay mare with a white blaze on her forehead. He was wearing a blue jean jacket and a black cowboy hat. I got out of the pickup and walked over to him.

"Well, boy," he said, "Glad to see you. How have you and Buddy been getting along?

"Just fine. I would have brought Buddy along, but I'm in kind of a hurry."

"Well, then, what brings you out here in the cold?"

"I need a place to burn a briefcase, Grandpa," I said.

"You want to burn a briefcase?"

"Yes."

"Well, take it down by the creek at the edge of the woods. You can find some nice dry limbs laying around there to build a fire with. Or you can take a few pieces off the woodpile and burn it right here if you want to."

"I'll take it down by the creek. No point using up your cut wood or making a mess in your yard."

"Mind if I go with you, Mikey."

"Glad to have you. Hop in."

He didn't exactly hop in, but he got in without any trouble, and I drove to the suggested place with the briefcase sitting on edge between us.

We got out and, sure enough, found enough windfall to gather a nice pile of dry limbs. I built it up in a bare spot and got it going with a generous portion of starter fluid. When the fire was burning well without my help, I brought the briefcase out of the truck and squirted the remaining can and a half of starter fluid over it. I let it soak for about a minute, and then I laid it on top of the burning logs. I had to jump back as the flames flared up from it.

Grandpa and I stood there and watched it wrinkle and shrivel in the flames. He drew as close as the heat would let him and peered at the burning valise as the fire ate it up, but there wasn't much to see because the contents seemed to have been mostly papers and they burned like crazy. I also caught a glimpse of some CDs. They could have been music, videos, or computer files. I guessed the last would be most likely.

Everything burned so fiercely that I suspected that Vince had packed wax or some other accelerant inside to make sure of complete destruction. When there was nothing left but the latches, hinges, and other small metal parts of the briefcase, I started kicking dirt on the fire and kept at it until it was safely out.

"We could have easy brought a shovel from the tool shed," Grandpa said, "I didn't think of it."

"Neither did I," I said, thinking I'd need to wipe my shoes when I got home.

When I stopped the truck at the house, Grandpa opened the door but hesitated before getting out.

"Mikey," he said, "I don't want to be nosey, but what was in that suitcase?"

"I'll be damned if I know."

"Oh."

He got out, shut the door and waved as I drove off.

CHAPTER 4
I GET THE BUSINESS

I had intended that no one know about a secret-laden briefcase at Vince Talbot's house. Now, his whole family and my grandfather knew about it. *Sorry, Vince, I did the best I could.* At least no one will ever know what it contained, and I guessed that was the important thing. At least, I hoped so. Looking back at everything that happened later, I wish I had fired up Vince's patio grill and had all the kinfolks watch me burn the damned thing.

The next morning at a little after nine-thirty, I got a call from Myra Pinkerton, Vince's sister from Dallas.

"Are you up?" she said.

"Sure," I said, "I'm usually up at this time."

"Well, Vince's lawyer is already here."

"About the will?"

"Yes. Aren't you coming?"

"Don't tell me I'm in it."

There was a pause, and then Myra continued a little coldly. "Vince told me he gave you a copy of the will. Haven't you read it?"

"No. I thought it was just a precaution, a backup copy. I didn't think the contents were any of my business."

"Well, get your . . . body over here."

I checked on Buddy. He was busy reading something on the Web, so I grabbed my copy of the will and headed out. I got there just as the reading was beginning. I didn't seem to be any more popular with the Talbot clan than I had been the previous morning. Raymond and Myra Pinkerton were friendly enough, as was Vince's father, and Vanessa gave me a warm smile, but the rest of the family seemed a little cool. Cool as in Alaska in January.

I took the seat Myra indicated, pulled out my copy of the will and started skimming. My God! Vince had left his business to me. *Why, Vince?* I didn't know anything about running a business. Vince had hardly discussed his business with me. I knew he did data analysis for oil and mining companies, and I thought he had some government research contracts, but I didn't know anything about that kind of thing. No wonder some of Vince's people had been a little hostile toward me. While I was mulling over these things the voice of the lawyer began to penetrate my consciousness.

Vince's lawyer wore the expected dark suit and tie. He was fairly young, not much over forty, I estimated, but he seemed to have no hair whatsoever on top of his head. A fringe of brown hair thrived in a horizontal crescent around the back of his head from one temple to the other, giving him the look of someone with a full head of hair that had been shaved neatly on top like a monk's tonsure. His name was Thomas Jackson, the same name as the famous Confederate general. He was calling the roll of beneficiaries and I duly answered when I heard my name.

I was still a little stunned about inheriting Vince's business, and this feeling was reinforced as I followed the reading with my copy and saw that the one Jackson was reading was exactly the same. After this confirmation I stopped reading along until I heard my name again.

". . . and all furniture, clothing, and other private property remaining in said house with the exception that Michael Kidd is to have all computers and related electronic equipment, filing cabinets with their contents, all the games and gaming devices, electric, electronic or mechanical and any portable containers, locked or unlocked, wherever they may be located within said house."

Well, that got me off the hook for removing the briefcase. It was mine anyway. *Why didn't you tell me to read the will, Vince?* If Paul had read a copy of the will, he would have known that. So why was he so testy about the briefcase?

The lawyer droned on. Myra was to dole out the furnishings among her father and siblings according to her discretion, and the house along with all his personal belongings, including his Porsche, was to be liquidated and divided equally among the tribe. Pretty simple, but it seemed that I was getting the lion's share. Then the kinfolks started asking questions about the assets. Paul was trying to pin the lawyer down.

"So how much, bottom line, am I going to get, Mr. Jackson?"

"I can't say exactly. It depends on how much the real estate sells for. Also, I don't yet know how much Mr. Talbot had in his safety deposit box. Or boxes. It may turn out that he has more than the one I know about."

"Give me a rough estimate."

"Well, assuming the house sells for its appraised value, and assuming nothing of value is found in your brother's safety deposit boxes, and that no other bank accounts or brokerage accounts turn up that I am not aware of now, I'd say—and this is just my guess—that each of you should get around ten million. I mean each of you who are named in the will except Mr. Kidd. He gets nothing but Mr. Talbot's share of the business and the items named. Most of his assets are in mutual funds so that ten million dollar estimate is also assuming the market doesn't crash before his stock portfolio is liquidated."

This left everyone, including me, speechless. I wouldn't have thought Vince was worth more than seven or eight million, including the business. His family apparently hadn't known Vince's material worth any more than I had. The epidemic of vocal paralysis didn't last long. Excitement spread across the room, and soon they were out of their chairs and chattering about their good fortune. Myra and Raymond were hugging each other. I went over to congratulate them, and Myra hugged me. Her facial expression kept alternating between joy and shame for the joy. I didn't blame her for either emotion. I was feeling a little strange myself.

I walked over to Vanessa.

"I had no idea Vince was so rich," I said.

"Neither did I. Neither did any of us. It's too bad Vince couldn't have lived longer. I'm sure he would have shared a lot of it with us, and we could have all enjoyed it together."

"One good thing for me, though. I'm off the hook for that briefcase."

"Uh-huh, you had every right to take it with you. I thought you knew that."

"Also, the family's getting so much they aren't going to begrudge my getting Vince's business."

"No, they won't. At first."

"What do you mean by that?"

"They won't resent it at first, but then they'll start to realize that all these millions were generated by the business. And you got the business."

I noticed Jackson beckoning to me, and when I approached he handed me a bulging manila envelope.

"This contains some keys and a couple of lock combinations at DataDigm, Incorporated. It will take a little time to re-register Mr. Talbot's stock in your name, but it's just a formality. I'll take care of it if you like."

I nodded and he went on. "Mr. Talbot owned sixty percent of the stock. Therefore he had complete control of its management. He was the

CEO and chairman of the board and, for practical purposes, he *was* the board. He had complete control of the corporation and, unless you decide to sell enough stock to leave you with 50 percent or less of the total, that power redounds to you."

Again I nodded and again he continued. "News of Mr. Talbot's death might cause a decline in the price of the stock, but that should be only a temporary effect as I understand that the corporation's income derives from long term contracts that are routinely renewed."

I waited for him to say something more, but he didn't. So I decided to drive over to the business location and look it over. I left Vince's house as soon as the reading was complete without waiting for all the questions to be fielded by the attorney. But once I got into the truck and began driving, it struck me that Vince was really dead. He was— had been—my best friend, and here I was racing over to see what I had gained from his death. I became ashamed, and then blue, bluer than I had been since my mother died. *Shit, Vince, I don't want your business. What I want is to see you again. Like you used to be, wry wit and fun and a pleasure to be with.*

I turned the pickup around and headed home.

CHAPTER 5
VINCE ALL OVER

They cremated Vince's body. I was still in a funk at the memorial service and figured I would be for awhile. We all have friends, and I've had a few that I really liked. But I've known only one that I could have called from anywhere, regardless of how far, tell him where I was and that I was in trouble, hang up without giving any information other than where I was calling from, and count on his showing up, as Grandpa liked to say, with a checkbook in one hand and a loaded pistol in the other, willing to use whichever was called for. No wonder I was blue. I would never have another friend like Vince.

Each of Vince's siblings said a few words at the service, but his father just sat and stared. Myra asked me to say something so I talked a little about Vince's love of puzzles and games. I didn't say so, but I had given up playing most board games with Vince because he treated them so seriously, dragging them out as he calculated the best conceivable moves. We continued to play chess, even in the hospital, because we used a chess clock that guaranteed the maximum time for a game. He was good at every kind of game, including, when he was well, athletic games like racket ball, tennis, and softball. His forte, though, was poker, and I couldn't hold a candle to him there.

I got a little laugh from the crowd when I said Vince played Monopoly as if the money were real and he played poker as if it were Monopoly money. But that was exactly the way it was with Vince. Everything was a game, and winning was everything.

When I sat down, the minister resumed his place at the lectern.

"Thank you," he said. "If no else wishes to say anything about the deceased, we will—"

"Wait a minute!" A small man hurried up the isle from the rear of the chapel. He wore a rumpled suit of light olive color. He bounced up the three steps to the platform and moved in between the minister and the microphone He looked out at the assembly, his head barely visible over the top of the lectern.

"What's going on here?" he said in a high pitched, nervous voice. "I can't believe this! You people don't know who you're honoring here! Only one of you mentioned poker, and Vince Talbot was a legend among poker players."

Then I recognized him. His name was Benny something. He was a professional dealer at one of Houston's highest stakes poker games. I had seen him there when Vince brought me along on several occasions. It was there that I discovered I wasn't cut out for high stakes poker, so I would usually stop playing after about an hour or until I had lost a previously decided amount. Vince would stay in for several hours and usually come out well ahead.

I would pass the time chatting with the owner of the game, who only played when one of the tables was short a player, and that was not often. Usually there were players waiting for a vacant chair. I looked toward the back of the chapel, and sure enough he was there, the man who ran one of the biggest games in the Houston area. The dealer had just called Vince a legendary figure, but this man truly was legendary among poker players. His name was Gar Paine, and he had a dignity about him befitting a man in his seventies. Slightly overweight, he used a heavy cane when rising and sitting down because he had left a portion of one leg in a foreign battlefield while serving in the United States Marine Corps. Although he walked well once he was on his feet, one of them was prosthetic.

Meanwhile, Benny the dealer was still nervously haranguing the audience about Vince's skill at poker, sprinkled with adventures that had occurred around Gar Paine's tables when Vince had been present and even some that had no bearing on Vince at all. I guess I didn't know Vince as well as I thought, or else Benny was exaggerating.

I knew Vince had considerable skill, but I was having a hard time thinking of him as someone with a national reputation as a truly great player. I decided Vince was somewhere in between my previous estimation and Benny's.

But the presence of Gar Paine was testimony to Vince's being a well-known player.

"There was the time—" Benny rattled on.

"Thank you, thank you." The minister said, taking advantage of the fact that Benny had turned loose of the lectern to gesture with both arms. He moved between the lectern and Benny and then turned to shake his hand, at the same time signaling to some unseen assistant to turn on the music. Benny was still talking but his words were drowned out by the Royal Scots Pipes and Fifes playing *Amazing Grace* at high volume. The minister, a large and well-built man, didn't turn loose of Benny's hand until he had walked him off the platform. I think the little dealer would have tried to go back except that he saw Gar Paine beckoning him back to his seat.

After the ceremony I mingled with the attendees, recognizing some by their faces but few by their names. I had seen a couple of men before in Vince's game room where he used to have a weekly low-stakes poker game. I remembered the name of one of them, Carl Hindman, a blond man of about fifty whom I knew to be one of Vince's employees.

"Is it true that you're taking Vince's place at DataDigm?" he said after we shook hands.

"Well, it's true that Vince left me his stock. What I'll do with it I haven't decided."

"If you decide to keep the stock and manage the company, you can count on my support."

"Carl, what is your job at DataDigm?"

"Like others of the old-time employees, I own stock in the company. My actual job is head of personnel and security. That's what I do now. When we first started I was an engineer. I worked with Vince on the first contracts we had. I was sort of the inside man—one of them— while Vince was the salesman. Of course, Vince was at that time heavily involved with the technical end as well."

He paused, I suppose to get my reaction. I didn't say anything, just nodded.

"I guess I'll see you soon at the plant?" he said.

"I expect to be out there early next week."

As I turned away Gar Paine walked up to me and extended his hand. "*Semper Fi,*" he said. That fraternal greeting is used by active, reserve, former, and retired marines to one another.

"*Semper Fi.* I didn't realize Vince was so famous as a poker player."

"Well, Benny was laying it on a little thick, as he usually does. But I'd say that most high stakes players in the Houston area knew him or knew him by reputation. And he was good. A good player and a good man, too. He could have made a fine living playing. He was a master of the psychological aspect of the game, and that's something that can't be taught. You either have it or you don't. It isn't just figuring the odds. A lot of people can do that. It's figuring the odds given what you've learned about how the other players think. You used to come with Vince to my place; you'd be welcome back at any time."

I thought, *and that's what makes you successful. You hustle your game wherever you are. And more power to you.*

"A lot of the players will miss Vince," he continued. "He used to talk about you a lot. In fact, you and I need to get together and talk about some unfinished business of Vince's in Houston—"

"Hey!" It was the excitable little dealer again. He hurried up to get into the conversation. "I remember you. You came with Vince sometimes to Gar's game. What's wrong with these people? You're the only one who gave Vince any credit for being a really great poker player. You're Mike Kidd, right?"

I was surprised Benny remembered my name. I knew Gar fairly well from having chatted with him several times, but I didn't remember ever saying much to Benny except "pass," "call," "fold," and "raise," the set phrases used to communicate with the dealer.

"So you really think Vince was one of the all time great poker players?" I said.

"Great? Listen, I've dealt to all the great poker players. They come from all over the country. Sooner or later they all come to Gar's game. I don't just deal, I study the players. I'm telling you they ought to spread Vince's ashes over all the poker tables in Houston."

"Maybe they ought to. But I hear that they're going to divide the ashes among his brothers and

40

sisters and I guess they'll take them off in different directions."

"Well," Gar said, "that's Vince all over."

CHAPTER 6
WHO'S IN CHARGE?

In the days following Vince's cremation I tried to get interested in the going business Vince had left me. It was located a couple of miles outside of town toward the west, and it would have been hard to find if I hadn't been there before. A dignified sign with the single word "DataDigm" set into an upright brick support divided the driveway going in from the one coming out. I drove up to the front of the building. I had never been inside, but I had picked Vince up right here more than once to drive us out to lunch. It was a single story modernistic structure of a few thousand square feet. There were parking spaces for dozens of cars but only about half were occupied. I saw the parking space with "Talbot" on it and pulled in.

I had met some of the staff at the services for Vince, but I didn't recognize the receptionist. She was a very thin brunette who managed to look attractive despite the fact that her curves were rather angular. She was wearing a badge that said "Antoinette Black."

"Can I help you?" she said.

"I'm sure you can. I'm the new owner of DataDigm. My name is Michael Kidd."

That did, indeed, get her attention. She stood up, offered her hand and introduced herself.

"It was sad about Vince," she said. "I guess I should show you around. But first I'll make you a visitor's badge."

"Well, I'm not exactly a visitor," I said. "I own the place."

"That's what I've heard," she said, smiling. "But we do some classified government work and their rules require both a visitor's badge and an escort if you want a tour of the whole place. The escort will be me. That's only for certain areas. After you get a government clearance, of course, you won't need an escort. You'll have your own badge showing your clearance level, and even though, as you say, you own the place, you'll still need the badge when you go into those classified areas."

She handed me a clip-on badge with "Visitor" printed across it. "Now," she said, "who do you want to see?"

"Whoever is in charge when Vince isn't here."

That seemed to stump her, so I said, "Who signs the checks?"

"The pay checks are issued automatically with facsimile signatures of Vince Talbot. It's all in the computers."

"Who hires new employees?"

"Vince. I mean he did, but we haven't hired a new employee in ages. We have a Director of Personnel but Vince always interviewed new hires and gave final approval before they came onboard."

"If you need office supplies, who okays that? Who pays for it?"

"Petty cash. If it's something expensive, then it would be Jim Martinez, the treasurer. He's also the accountant."

"Okay," I said, "take me to him or have him come up. He can show me around."

"He's not here today."

I was feeling a little frustrated. "Well, get me whoever can tell me about how this business operates."

She came around from behind the counter, smiled a little lamely and said, "Follow me."

"Well, can't you summon someone else to escort me? I hate to take you away from the reception area."

"That's all right. Visitors are rare, and almost everyone who shows up for business purposes has an appointment. I'll take you to Mr. Hindman. He's been here forever and can explain everything much better than I."

"Carl Hindman, the security man? I know him. I used to see him at Vince's poker game. And he was at Vince's memorial."

"Good, you know him. He's also the Personnel man. He'll be glad to show you around."

"What about the phone? Is it all right for you to leave it?"

"It'll be all right. It takes messages."

Vince's business wasn't fitting the bustling picture I had imagined. "Lead on," I said.

She seemed to understand my confusion. "There's not enough coming and going to justify a full-time receptionist. I do tech editing and other jobs. I'm actually more of a secretary than a receptionist."

She led and I followed. But she hadn't answered my real question. How could a company that couldn't keep a receptionist busy provide Vince with a net profit of a hundred million dollars or more over the period of about fifteen years? We went down a long corridor with offices on both sides. The doors had no names or descriptions, no words at all, just little brass plates with numbers on them.

"Who are in these offices?"

"Nobody, now. There used be a much larger staff, and these offices were used mostly by engineers, senior engineers. There were lots more engineers in the cubicle area ahead."

We came upon and entered a cavernous, high-ceilinged room filled with fabric covered partitions about seven feet tall that divided the space into small offices. Each was furnished with two chairs, a filing cabinet, a desk, and a large computer monitor. Closed laptop computers sat on some of the desks. We passed several empty cubicles while the sinking feeling in my gut grew worse. Finally, we came to an occupied cubicle. Carl Hindman looked up from the laptop keyboard he was pecking at.

"Carl," Antoinette said. "I believe you know Mr. Kidd, the new owner. Mr. Kidd, I'm going to turn you over to Carl."

As Carl and I shook hands Antoinette left us and headed back the way we came.

"So you want to see what Vince got you into," Carl Hindman said.

"Antoinette said you know more about it than anyone."

"Maybe not more, but at least as much," he said. "I was one of the company's first employees. There were over a hundred of us at the high point of employment. I saw the birth and growth of this company. I hope I'm not about to witness its death."

"Is it drying up that fast?"

"No, it's not drying up at all. As far as I know the company is still sound. I mean I don't know what you, as the new owner, have in mind. All these empty offices are partly the result of the company's policy of allowing employees to work off-site and to choose their own hours. The ones working on classified government contracts all still work on-site. Come on and I'll give you the Cook's tour. Did Antoinette show you Vince's office?"

When I shook my head, he led me part way back along the route I had already traveled. We came to a door marked simply "9." Carl swung it open with a flourish. The room was quite large and lined with bookcases. The floor was carpeted. The desk was big and walnut. Everything was about as you would expect for the office of the CEO of a successful business—except for the toys.

There were several of those science gimmicks on the desk, the little pendulums that demonstrate conservation of momentum, various magnetic gadgets that, once started, move in strange patterns. There was even a Rubik's Cube. Mixed in among the books on the shelves were dozens of wire, wooden, rope, and plastic puzzles. All these reminded me of Vince and his insatiable fascination with games and puzzles. The crowning ornament was a large square wall clock of the Monopoly game board. The little capitalist trademark figure was pointing out the time with his hands, his walking cane extending one arm to make the minute hand.

"In some ways," I said, "this looks more like a play room than an office."

"Vince did love his toys. But he knew how to work, too. When I would come in here he usually was pounding away at the keyboard or drawing diagrams on a green pad. But sometimes he would be idly fooling with one of these puzzles. I think that he used them to stimulate his thinking. In other words, even when he was toying with one of these puzzles he was thinking about serious things."

"Suppose I decide to take over where Vince left off?"

"Big shoes to fill, but I guess Vince thought you could do it or he wouldn't have left you the business. If you're seriously contemplating running the company we probably should start the ball rolling by getting a SECRET clearance. Otherwise you won't be able to even read the reports done for the army, and that's a significant part of our work although the major income is from unclassified data analysis for industrial clients."

"And you're the security man."

"Right. I'll get you a stack of forms and set up an interview with the FBI. Then it's just a matter of waiting a few weeks while they make their investigations. You were in the military, right? That will help speed things up as they already have a lot of information about you."

"Yeah, the Marine Corps."

I moved around behind Vince's desk and sat down in his heavy-duty swivel chair. I motioned Carl to sit down in one of the chairs facing the desk. I wanted to break away from the informal both-friends-of-Vince to a more formal but still friendly employer-employee relationship.

"All right, Carl," I said, "Tell me everything I need to know about DataDigm."

* * *

I learned a lot from Carl that day, but not enough to satisfy me as to how the business could have brought in so much money. He said that the weekly poker game that Vince used to host was still going on, but now the job of hosting it rotated among the players. The one coming up was at Carl's house and he invited me to join in.

I hesitated for a moment because I had always heard that the boss should remain slightly aloof from the employees. But this corporation was built by Vince, apparently on a first name basis with plenty of social contact between Vince and at least the upper management. I thought I'd better stick with Vince's methods as far as I could and besides, I needed to get to know the managers in a hurry if I was going to keep the job I had inherited. So I agreed to go the next Friday evening to Carl's house.

CHAPTER 7
DEAL ME IN

By closing time on Friday Carl Hindman had reminded me twice of my promise to attend the poker game at his house. By then I had met most of the upper and middle management team of DataDigm and knew that some of them would be there. Carl lived in a fairly new two story house in a community with a brick wall around it and gates that closed at night and had to be operated with a code, which Carl had given me.

I had expected to meet Carl's wife, but it was Carl who opened the door at my ring. I found out as the evening wore on that Carl and his wife had separated and he expected her to file for divorce. He didn't say when she had moved out, but the furniture arrangement and decor still spoke of a woman's touch, so I guessed it hadn't been long.

The poker table had been set up in the family room, and Carl had set out snacks, cheese dip and corn chips, and nuts. The table was like the one at Vince's house, octagonal with pockets set into the rim to hold drinks.

"There's beer in the kitchen fridge," Carl said, pointing toward a door.

Besides Carl there were three other players present, although play had not yet begun. I hadn't asked, but I had assumed that all the players would be company men. And so they were. I had already met two of them at work. They were Jack McKinney and Jack Hinton, the two senior executives that headed up the military and industrial sections, respectively. The third man was Jim Martinez, the elusive accountant and treasurer. He kept irregular hours and I had not had a chance to meet him before.

"So there really is a Jim Martinez," I said.

He laughed. "Yeah, I guess I should have come by the shop to meet you. I was going to but somehow kept putting it off. I don't work by the hour, as I assume you know. You'll see a lot of me around the first of each month when I do an audit and write checks. You'll soon see more of me than you probably will want because tax time is approaching."

He was a good looking man in his thirties with a full head of dark brown hair with some gray in his temples and moustache. As the evening wore on I learned to respect his quick mind. He always knew whose deal it was, who was in, whose turn to ante and how much, and all the sundry facts needed to keep the game running smoothly.

The deal rotated and the game was dealer's choice. Since there were only five of us, most variations of poker could be played, and several were before we settled down to Hold 'Em, the most popular game played in casinos. Its popularity arose from the fact that many players could be accommodated at a single table because the up-cards were common to all the players.

According to Gar Paine, it started long ago in Robstown, Texas, and became standard all over the country in a few years. I like it fine when the deal stays with one man who doesn't play, but when it rotates keeping up with the antes gets a bit tedious. Jim took on that chore without a problem and apparently with no effort. I hoped that meant he was a good accountant.

The stakes were low for men of their income level, which suited me because I was more interested in learning about my business team than I was in the game, and high limit bets always force me to concentrate on the cards. Besides, although I was technically rich, nothing had yet made its way into my bank account. I was still thinking as a man of modest means. I expected that would begin to change with the first paycheck I would draw from DataDigm at the end of the month. Even then, I knew that it would take several months for me to change my mindset. My newly acquired wealth was tied up in the company and I was still pondering on whether to dump my stock and be a rich retiree or to become something I really didn't feel was true to my character, namely a business executive.

I felt that my presence was inhibiting conversation. I was the new boss and they still didn't know what to expect from me. How could they? I hadn't yet made up my mind on whether to permanently take on the role that Vince had thrust on me. There wasn't a lot of conversation at first, but after several hands had been played and everyone had consumed a couple of beers along with snacks, the social aspects of the game began to appear. Off-color jokes went around the table and little jabs of irony passed between the members of the group, most of which were insider things lost on me.

"Would anybody like to tell me where the name DataDigm came from?" I said during a lull.

"I never liked it myself," Jim said. "I thought it was 'data, dig 'em?' until I came to work there. If they wanted to call it 'data dime' why didn't they spell it that way?"

Jack McKinney said, "Very funny. I suppose you never heard of the word that means a typical example or a model for something, *paradigm*. Or do you pronounce that para dig 'em?"

Jack Hinton said, "That's what our siggen says." And then he laughed heartily at his own joke.

"I'm afraid I had a hand in that," Carl said. "We were 'Talbot Analyses' at first. Then we wanted something high-tech sounding and Vince wanted his name out with the idea of eventually selling the company or going public. We wanted something to convey data analysis. I thought of Paradigm Data, and we shortened it down to DataDigm. It seems to work okay."

One thing about low stake poker games, they tend to be chatty. So it didn't seem to be improper for Jim Martinez to suddenly ask me, "Where did you graduate, Mike, and what is your degree in?"

I glanced at Carl without thinking. He was processing my clearance and had all the details of my background including the fact that I had no degree at all. I wondered what he had shared with others, if anything. Surely, disclosing anything would be inconsistent with the protocol of his job. He looked back at me and shook his head negatively a tiny bit.

I looked back at Martinez. "I graduated from Robert E. Lee High School. I don't have a degree in anything."

The pause in chatter was long enough to be awkward. Of the various kinds of snobbery with which I have become acquainted that of the degreed versus the non-degreed is the one I dislike the most. I'd already noticed that the DataDigm engineers never fraternized with the lowly machinists who transformed their ideas into realities.

Grandpa never finished high school, but he is broadly read and knows more about history and world geography than most college graduates. He claims that the high school graduate of his generation was better educated than today's college graduate. I was with him several years ago on a deer hunt with several others when he remarked that he had read a news report that said that most university students couldn't identify the nation of Portugal on an unlabeled world map.

"I'm not surprised," one of the hunters had said. "I graduated college and medical school, and

I consider myself to be an educated man. I doubt that I could find Portugal on a map."

Grandpa was never noted for diplomacy even when he was trying to be tactful. "Well, I'm sure you are a competent surgeon and know everything you need to know in your profession. You are doubtless very well trained. *Trained!* But a person that can't find Portugal on a map in *not* educated."

Carl Hindman broke the silence. "I hope you don't mind, Mike, if I mention that you have enough college credits for more than one degree, but never took some of the prerequisites to graduate."

Carl's remark seemed to restore about half of my prestige.

I can't say that I had learned a lot about the business by the time the game broke up about 1 a.m. but I had learned something about the personalities of the upper management.

Jim Martinez, our treasurer and accountant, was a little aloof but impressed me as highly intelligent and entirely competent. Jack McKinney seemed sharp and on top of the government contract work, a no-nonsense type who would see that things were done right. Jack Hinton must be competent because he had been managing the big money seismic data analysis contracts that accounted for most of the corporate income. But he hadn't brought in any new contracts in years, and I would have to find out why. It seemed to me that he and Carl Hindman might both be coasting. As head of personnel, Carl had little to do in the way of adding or subtracting employees, there just wasn't much going on there. As head of security he had to keep things straight with the military contracts. That might have taken more effort than I could so far see. I wondered if his marital problems might be impacting his work.

I did feel a little better about the soundness of DataDigm. It was not on the decline as it initially seemed to me. The vacant offices and lack of customer traffic were due to changes that had resulted in fewer people doing more expensive work. The company used to have more personnel because originally it depended on many small contracts. Now it appeared that most of the money came from a few large contracts that required few analysts.

This was especially true for the non-military work where Vince had apparently sold several large oil and mining firms on continually analyzing their seismic data. So now I saw where the money was coming from. All I needed to know was what DataDigm was doing for these companies that was worth millions annually.

One thing I did learn about my managers. None of them was much good at poker. I almost had to force myself not to wind up the big winner for the night. I thought that would be a management mistake on my part.

As I shook hands before leaving Jim Martinez said, "Well one thing is different about you from

Vince. He used to take back part of our salaries every game. I don't think he ever left as a loser."

That was typical of Vince. Even with low stakes, even with no stakes, he played to win and he played hard. And apparently even when it might be to his disadvantage. *Vince, I miss you.*

Driving back home I had a feeling of satisfaction. I was getting a handle on the business I had inherited, and getting to know the key people I would be working with. Those people were turning out to be friendly and personable. I liked them all. How was I to guess that one of them would soon try to kill me?

CHAPTER 8
IT'S HER CALL

"All right, Carl," I'd said, "Tell me everything I need to know about DataDigm." That sentence had been so productive that I used it three more times with other names beside Carl. The company structure was a simple division between the government contracts and the industry contracts, and I had summoned the heads of those departments, Jack McKinney and Jack Hinton, separately and asked the same question. That question also came in handy with the company accountant, Jim Martinez.

I now was beginning to get a grasp on what was going on at my inherited company. The appearance that no one was in charge was the result of Vince's prolonged illness. He set things to run on autopilot. Besides that, he apparently had always operated on a delegated responsibility concept.

Now that I was involved, I remembered Vince's talking occasionally about his management philosophy. He didn't have a sales department; there was no product to sell other than mathematical analysis. Any company engineer or mathematician was authorized to represent the company in calling on potential clients. Anyone who brought in a contract was made contract manager for that project. If he brought in more than one contract, he could appoint managers for each of the contracts.

Travel expenses were generous for those wishing to visit prospects. All that was required was that the idea be explained to Vince and approved by him. If the idea excited Vince he often went with the employee to help nail down the contract.

Vince's model had worked well for the first few years of DataDigm's existence, but the initial fast growth had slowed to a mere holding pattern, and this was long before Vince's health hit its final, fatal decline. It was as if Vince had reached the level of business he desired and had stopped pushing for more customers. To allow every engineer to be a salesman had worked, I suspected, because Vince was really the sales department. In my experience the best technical people were introverts whereas the best salesmen were extroverts. It must be rare to find someone who is really good at both. My appreciation for Vince's abilities grew the more I learned about the company.

Carl Hindman and a few other long-term company men were minor stock holders. That included Jim Martinez, the treasurer and accountant. These men had taken small salaries with stock options, and had done well when the corporation went public. Vince had sold quite a bit of his stock when its price shot up on going public. That would account for some of his wealth, but not nearly all of it.

About two weeks after my first visit to DataDigm headquarters, I was sitting at Vince's big walnut desk, which was piled high with the reports to our customers—mainly the industrial reports because most of the government reports were classified and I still didn't have the necessary clearances—when Antoinette Black signaled that I had a telephone call. I picked up with, "Mike Kidd here."

"Hi, Mike, this is Vanessa Talbot."

An image immediately flashed in my mind of Vince's kid sister. Dark hair, big moist brown eyes, and kissable lips. I was surprised to realize she had made that much of an impression on me at the time. She had helped me get the briefcase out of Vince's house, but I had not thought of her in the weeks since.

"Hey, Vanessa. It's a pleasure to hear from you."

"I'm glad. What are you up to?"

"I'm sitting here at Vince's desk wearing my DataDigm badge trying to make heads and tails out of these statistical analyses reports that Vince got so much money for."

"Well, when are you going to come pick up your stuff?"

"I didn't know I had any stuff in Missouri."

"I'm in Tyler, silly. I'm at Vince's house. Did you forget that all these electronic games and stuff are yours?"

"By George, I did forget. Why don't I come pick you up for lunch?"

"Why don't you come on over while I fix something here."

"I wouldn't trust any of the groceries there," I said. "They're getting pretty old."

"I've moved in. I've just gone grocery shopping. Are you coming?"

"I'm on the way. See you in a few minutes."

Vanessa opened the door before I had time to ring the bell. It seemed a little strange being in Vince's home again. Vanessa had hot taco meat and shells set out on the kitchen bar along with cheese, salsa, lettuce, chopped tomatoes, and chopped onions. We made tacos to our individual tastes and she took a couple of cold beers out of the refrigerator.

"I already know who you are," she said as we loaded our warm taco shells. "You don't need to show me your badge."

"Damn!" I said as I unclipped it and tucked it into my pocket. "First I can't remember to put it on and then I can't remember to take it off. How did you know I like tacos?"

"Who doesn't? Besides, I figured if you didn't we could still go out."

And so we had our first meal together. I hoped there would be more because I found myself very much enjoying being with her. At first we tried to shorten the inevitable pauses that come when making small talk, but then we began to let them happen while we munched away at our tacos and smiled at each other.

"So you just up and quit your job and moved to Tyler?" I said.

"Wouldn't you quit a job you didn't like if you could afford to?"

"It's the story of my life. I've never held a job for very long, except the Marines. They won't let you quit until your enlistment is up. You see, I get oil royalties from my mother's lease. The income is not enough to make me a playboy, but it has given me the independence to stop working when the job gets boring or the boss gets insulting. I get just enough oil money to live modestly without working, but I usually work for somebody a few months out of the year to accrue some extra bucks."

She seemed to think about that for a few seconds. Then she said, "Of course I haven't received any of Vince's money yet. But I have some savings. Mr. Jackson says there's no reason I shouldn't live in Vince's house until it's sold. I guess I could buy it from the estate if I want to and just live here from now on."

"I wish you would. I like the idea of seeing you often."

"Well, you just happen to be the only person in Tyler I know so I hope we will be seeing each other at least until I meet a few other people. Well, I know Mr. Jackson, the lawyer, and I've met a couple of others but you know what I mean."

"When word gets around that you're rich you won't have any problem meeting people. In the meantime I'll make the sacrifice of devoting myself to showing you the cultural high points, the effervescent night life and the magnificent natural wonders of East Texas."

"And what do you think we should do first?"

"First, I'm going to introduce you to high society, starting tonight with my own family," I said, wondering why I was saying it. Then I knew. *Let's get the sticking point over with first. Let's find out right away if she can take Buddy.*

CHAPTER 9
A MOOT QUESTION

When I got back to DataDigm Antoinette told me I had a visitor waiting in my office.

"How long has he been waiting?"

"Almost an hour. I suggested he come back or set up an appointment, but he said he would wait. I put him in your office. I hope that's all right. I gave him a visitor's badge and told him not to leave without an escort. He's been here before. His name is Van Moot, spelled with a double-o but pronounce *Mote*."

When I opened the door, Van Moot was standing next to a bookcase toying with one of Vince's wire puzzles. He was a heavy-set man in his sixties, with close-cropped hair of blond mixed with gray. His suit of blue with white pinstripes was obviously tailor-made and perfectly fitted to his stocky body. He had a Van Dyke style mustache and beard that would have looked much better of a thinner face.

"Mr. Van Moot?" I said, extending my hand. "I'm Mike Kidd."

He looked at me closely while shaking my hand firmly.

"I'm pleased to meet you, Mr. Kidd. We were very sad to learn of Mr. Talbot's death. I understand that you are taking his place."

"Yes." I moved around to the chair behind Vince's desk and motioned him to take a seat. "What can I do for you?"

As he sat down he took a small silver box from his pocket and extracted a business card, which he handed me. Under *Hendrik Van Moot* was the company name, which I recognized from some of the reports I had been studying and which were still piled on the desk.

"I see that you represent one of our most valued customers," I said.

"I would presume so. We have been doing business for a good many years." The address on his business card was New York, but his English was flavored with a slight accent I guessed to be South African rather than Holland Dutch. That would be consistent with a mining company. "I have come to be reassured that our business relationship has not been altered in any way since Mr. Talbot's demise."

"The only change in personnel is that I have taken Mr. Talbot's place as manager and principal owner of the company. The same analysts are still here and they are using the same computer programs. The quality of the analyses will not be affected in the slightest."

"I was speaking about the contractual obligations of all parties."

He paused as if expecting reassurance. I hadn't read the contract with his company but I sure as hell would as soon as he left. In the meantime I couldn't think of any reason there would be a change with Vince's death, so I said, "Everything will continue exactly as it has in the past."

"And you understand the consequences of failure on your part to uphold your side of the contract?"

His company was one of several that were important to the income flow of DataDigm, and I took what he said as a threat to cut off that money stream. I didn't like his tone, but he was an important customer who was saying—that's what I thought at the time—he would cut us off if we let down on the timeliness or quality of our work.

"You have my assurance," I said, "that everything will continue exactly as before Mr. Talbot died."

With that Van Moot got to his feet and extended his hand. We shook hands and I signaled Antoinette to come escort him to the front. As they left my office he turned back to me.

"By any chance did Mr. Talbot leave any papers for me?"

"I haven't come across any. If I do I will, of course, see that you get them."

As the door closed behind them I saw as in a vision a briefcase flaming in a wood fire on Grandpa's farm.

CHAPTER 10
FIRST DATE

It was 6 p.m. when I left DataDigm to pick up Vanessa. I had read the contract with Van Moot's company several times and saw only one thing that seemed unusual. The contract was to terminate on a date about five years from now in the future with no provision for renewal, and we were to give over to Van Moot's company all pertinent computer programs and documentation. All other relevant material or devices not already destroyed were to be delivered or destroyed.

Destroyed, as in burned up in a briefcase? I wondered. *And devices? What devices?* The analyses were all done mathematically.

By 6:30 Vanessa was seated beside me in the pickup and we were headed for Grandpa's. If he had followed my instructions he would have picked up both Buddy and four pounds of hot barbecued beef brisket with buns and fixings. If Tyler had plenty of anything it was Mexican food and Texas style barbecue, and all the restaurants specializing in those two foods were good. It was still March and a little chilly. Vanessa was dressed in jeans, a blue and white checkered shirt, and a tan leather jacket as I had told her what kind of informal dinner was on the agenda.

What I hadn't told her was anything about Buddy.

"Is your brother married," Vanessa asked.

There it was. I had been arguing with myself whether to tell her anything about Buddy. I thought maybe I would just introduce him and let her discover his problems for herself, and judge by her reactions whether there could be any chance for a lasting relationship for the three of us. Now it seemed best to warn her about what to expect.

"Buddy will never marry," I said.

"Another confirmed bachelor? Does it run in the family?"

"No, Buddy won't marry because he has no sexual passion. He's autistic. I don't know if that is common to autistic people, but Buddy seems absolutely immune to sexual feelings."

Vanessa didn't say anything, so I plunged on. "He doesn't seem to notice any differences between men and women. They're all just people to him, and not very interesting. His interests are mostly in inanimate things. He is fantastic at math. He memorized some complicated mathematical procedure that lets him calculate the day of the week for any date. Tell him your date of birth and he will tell you almost immediately the day of the week you were born. He is what they used to call an idiot-savant," I said. I wanted her to hear the word. "Now they say 'autistic-savant' as if words changed facts."

"Well, *idiot* is a pejorative word. And it's way too general. Can Buddy read?"

"It's his favorite thing. And he can quote most of it word for word."

"Does he live with your Grandfather?"

There it was again. *Let's get it over with.* "No. He lives with me."

She didn't say anything. I hadn't expected her to. I went on. "He stays with Grandpa sometimes for a few days when I'm out of town, but Grandpa is pushing ninety so it is inevitable that eventually Buddy will have to live with me, so a few years ago I moved him in with me. He's not helpless; he can dress himself and carry on a limited conversation. But he has to be told what to do or he will just read or count the shingles on a roof or otherwise neglect little things like taking a shower."

"Can he be left alone?"

"Yes, and I do that for hours at a time. But he can't be left alone for days. I usually come home a couple of times during the day to make sure he has eaten something and hasn't hurt himself. I try to keep cold cuts and sandwich material in the refrigerator. I don't trust him to cook or even open cans. But he often just forgets to eat, doesn't seem to get hungry unless you remind him. Then his appetite seems okay. We eat a lot of hamburgers. I bring them home with me. He is presentable in restaurants and his manners are not bad, but I cut up his steaks for him. I hope he doesn't disgust you."

"What a cruel thing to say! You shouldn't be ashamed of him."

"He's my brother and I love him. I just don't want you to be unpleasantly surprised."

It was dark and cold when we walked from my truck up to Grandpa's front porch. I opened the door without knocking and held it for Vanessa. Grandpa and Buddy were in the dining room setting the table. When he saw Vanessa, Grandpa immediately switched on the charm.

"Mikey, you shoulda warned us you were bringing a beauty queen. I would've bought some champagne and caviar." He stuck out his hand toward Vanessa. "Unless Mikey got confused with all his female friends, you must be Vanessa. I'm delightful to meet you."

"And unless Mike forgot to tell me he had more than one handsome and refined elderly gentleman in the family, you must be Grandpa."

"Actually, my name is Tom. But a gal as pretty as you can call me anything she likes and as often as she wants."

"Call him anything but 'Shorty'," I said. "He hits people that call him that."

"I'll call him Tom. Is it Tom Kidd?"

"No, I'm Mikey's mother's father. Last name is Foster. I'm Mikey's Foster grandfather, so to speak. And this here is Buddy, Mikey's younger brother."

"I'm glad to meet you, Buddy," Vanessa said, extending her hand. Buddy took it—thank God!—

held it for a moment and released it. He hardly looked at her.

"I was born on November 15, twenty-eight years ago," she said.

Now Buddy looked at her closely and smiled. "You were born on Thursday."

"That's right! How do you do that?"

"I just do it."

"There's an algorithm for it, but Buddy likes to look at calendars. I'm not sure whether he remembers or calculates."

"I just do it," Buddy said.

"What's 52 times 7," Vanessa said.

"Three-hundred and sixty-four."

"I know that's right. That's the days in a year minus one, 52 weeks of 7 days."

And that was the beginning of the relationship between Vanessa and Buddy. She never left him out of the conversation for long. Every few minutes she would ask him some math question. Usually, she had no way of checking on the answer but smiled anyway and said, "That's right." One time she gave him her phone number and her Social Security number without asking him to do anything with them.

"Hold on," I said. "Buddy, Vanessa's phone number and her Social Security number are private. Don't give them to anyone else. You hear?"

"I hear,' Buddy said. "I won't."

Vanessa seemed to be at home with Grandpa and Buddy. We all ate heartily, but there was enough brisket left over for Grandpa to save for a couple of later meals. I left Buddy with Grandpa for the night just in case something romantic developed between Vanessa and me. Before we left Vanessa said, "Buddy, what's my phone number and my Social Security number?"

He repeated them exactly, as I knew he would. She gave him a parting hug, and he smiled.

When I walked her to the door of Vince's house she didn't invite me in, but she did give me one hell of a goodnight kiss. I was right about those lips.

"What made you think that Buddy might disgust me?" she said before closing the door. "He's a very sweet person."

"Oh, lots of people can't stand to be around the mentally impaired."

"Like who?"

"Like my father. He left my mother because of it. He deserted my mother, me and Buddy. The son-of-a-bitch!"

She paused. I think she wanted to talk about it. But I didn't, so I turned and walked back to the truck.

CHAPTER 11
FOREWARNED

I don't have a college degree of any kind, but that was not because I hadn't earned one. I had taken most of the math courses available at both Tyler Junior College and the local branch of the University of Texas, including graduate courses. The only reason I don't have a bachelor's degree in math is because I never got around to taking the required nonmathematical courses. I kept thinking I would get around to that, but time passes and there is no urgency when you really don't have to work for a living.

The point is I know enough about statistics to see that something didn't add up with the Van Moot account. The inescapable conclusion was that, in the first place, DataDigm was overcharging the client for the work done, and that, in the second place, the client had to be aware of that fact.

The real work had been in the very first job done. That's when the computer program had been written to take data from the mining company's seismic recordings and turn them into graphs that the geologists could use to predict what lay beneath the surface of the earth. The methodology seemed advanced and the summary graphs looked as if they would be useful. The result of that first run may have been priced reasonably although it seemed very high. It included our converting their analog recordings to digital input for our computer program to process. We didn't actually make any predictions, that job was passed back to their geologists. We just made it easier for them to draw their own conclusions.

But the next job and every subsequent job had been priced at the same rate, although no further computer programming was done. We had just run it through the same program and produced the same kind of graphs, tables, and charts as before. Even the write-ups were virtually unchanged, boiler plate extracted from the first report. Of course, the graphs and tables generated were particular to the data supplied by the client. By the third job, they were even providing the input tapes already digitized. It was almost like free money.

I was studying the contract with Van Moot's company again when he called. I was wondering why his name didn't appear anywhere in the contract or in the sign-off of the reports on each job of statistical analysis we had done. Neither did his name appear anywhere on the company's website. His card was still on my desk—just his name above the company name. When Antoinette told me he was on the line, I decided to ask him exactly what his job was. I never got the chance.

"Mr. Van Moot, it's good to hear from you again."

"I'll get right to the point, Mr. Kidd. We have reason to believe that you may have broken your side of our bargain. Certain, shall we say, products proprietary to us have made their appearance in the general market."

I was dumbfounded. After a pause, Van Moot continued. "I hope that I am making myself clear."

"Not entirely. Are you saying that we revealed the analytical reports to your competitors?"

"Not the reports. Fuck the reports. I'm saying that Mr. Talbot had certain knowledge about our products that he fastidiously kept to himself as long as he was alive. Knowledge that could be very disadvantageous to us if not carefully kept under guard. Now Mr. Talbot is gone and you have taken his place. And now it appears that that knowledge has been carelessly revealed."

"Any such knowledge died with Mr. Talbot. I don't know what you're talking about."

"It seems it didn't die with him. He promised to destroy it. Do you know anything about the destruction of any of Mr. Talbot's papers? Any documents or devices?"

Oh shit, I thought, *the briefcase.*

"Well, Mr. Kidd, do you?"

"As a matter of fact, Vince left me a note telling me to burn a briefcase upon his death. I did so the day after he died. I burned it utterly and completely."

"Did you look through the contents? Did you remove anything?"

"No."

"Why not?"

"Vince asked me not to."

Now Van Moot seemed speechless. After a long pause he said, "You will pardon my skepticism, Mr. Kidd. I don't know whether you are responsible for the apparent leak or whether you even know what I am referring to, and I really don't care. The fact is you had that knowledge in your possession. You are the last person known to have had it and now it appears to have been compromised. We hold you responsible and you had better come up with a good explanation or face very severe consequences."

"Meaning you are planning on bringing a lawsuit against DataDigm?"

For the first time I heard Van Moot laugh, and I didn't like the sound of it. He hung up without saying another word.

CHAPTER 12
FOREARMED

Van Moot's sarcastic laughter played over and over in my mind. Surely he was not making a threat on my life. Or was he? I hadn't kept a loaded gun in the house for years because of Buddy. At one time I did keep a 9 mm autoloader in the nightstand next to my bed until I came in one afternoon and found Buddy busily taking it apart and reassembling it like a Rubik Cube puzzle. He had even been unloading and reloading the clip magazine. Thank God it didn't occur to him to fire the weapon.

Although I was pretty sure Buddy would leave it alone if I asked him to, I just didn't like the idea of leaving a gun there when I was out of the house. I could have put a trigger lock on it, but a pistol you couldn't immediately fire didn't seem worth having, so I had taken it out to Grandpa's and left it with him. But now it might be Buddy's life as well as mine on the line, and I was just going to have to lay the law down to him about even touching it.

As soon as I pulled up in his yard, Grandpa came out the front door. He was holding a bundle wrapped in a blanket, which I figured was my handgun, but instead of handing it to me he walked around and got into the passenger's seat.

"You coming with me, Grandpa?"

"Yeah. I got my old army .45 in here, too. Thought I might as well get my own license while we're at it."

That surprised me. Grandpa had always maintained that the U.S. Constitution was the only license he needed, and that applying for a license was admitting that carrying a gun was not a right but a privilege. To him it was like saying everyone had the right to free speech but that you had to get a license before you said anything controversial.

"It seems like you've changed your mind," I said.

"Hell no! I still feel the same way. But now it's not just my own ass I got to worry about. You and Buddy may need me to come running and I don't want some smart aleck deputy stopping me before I get there."

I didn't say anything. Grandpa didn't ever tell anyone he loved them, not in so many words. But he had just told me as near as he could bring himself to do it, and I was touched.

There were about thirty of us in the class. I was surprised to see that more than half were women. Ages went from late twenties up to late fifties, not counting Grandpa. So there was about a thirty year jump from the oldest of the others to Grandpa. You couldn't get a concealed carry license without taking several hours of instruction, and during the lectures you had to leave your firearm on the counter outside the classroom.

The pistols were sitting on top of the applications, and when Grandpa left his Model 1911 Colt .45 it stood out like a turkey in a chicken yard. It was twice the size and three times the weight of the other weapons. It was not only the oldest model weapon—Model 1911 stands for the year it was first produced for the Army—it was the oldest weapon in actual age, Grandpa having had it as long as I can remember. Of course, Grandpa stood out himself because of his age.

One of the instructors picked up Grandpa's pistol and sighted while pointing it toward the wall. He looked as if his full-time job might be in law enforcement. He was muscular and overweight, as so many policemen are; *burly* is the word. He looked to be about forty and had a thick moustache.

"You might want to replace the sights with something newer. You can hardly sight through this narrow notch."

"That's all right," Grandpa said. "My eyes aren't good enough to use the sights, anyway."

The instructor pursed his lips as if he was trying to think of something to say, but we walked on into the classroom before he could come up with anything.

There was another official already in the classroom, and the instructions were about to begin. The state of Texas requires the course to last seven hours, but everything that needs to said about shooting and gun safety can be covered in about two hours, so there was a lot of padding. This man looked like a younger, slightly thinner version of the first instructor. I guessed that this one would do the talking and the other one would do the firing range work. After drawing out the safety lecture and then telling us about the legal aspects of concealed carry, he finally drew his own weapon.

"Now some of you may be used to the old, one-handed way of firing a pistol," the instructor said, smiling at Grandpa. "But you'll get the best results with the combat stance in which you crouch like this and give additional support to the weapon with your other hand like this."

Grandpa seemed to be hanging on his every word and nodding at appropriate times. After about another hour of talk and demonstration, the instructor dismissed us for lunch. The Oh Susanna Restaurant was only a short walk away, and most of the class headed there. Grandpa seemed to be the class pet, and several people chatted with him as we walked. He is naturally outgoing and a clever talker, but once inside the café he steered me to a corner booth where we could talk privately.

"Just who is it that's after you, Mikey?" he said.

"I don't know for sure that anyone is, Grandpa. If there is I think it has to do with that briefcase I burned at your place. I'm glad you came for the course—"

I stopped talking because the waitress had come up to get our order. She was in her late fifties and no looker, but Grandpa immediately started flirting with her, and she flirted right back. Since he looks years younger than his age, she might have actually considered the flirting might lead to a date.

Flirting was just a habit with Grandpa, but I sometimes wonder what he does if he gets a serious positive response instead of the usual repartee. If the waitress thought he was twenty years younger than his age, then the folks in the shooting class probably thought the same thing. They would really be impressed if they knew he was almost ninety.

I ordered a chicken-fried steak and iced tea. Grandpa told her, "I'll have the same thing as my brother." She looked back and forth between us and then quizzically at Grandpa, and he laughed and so did she. If he'd have said "son" she would have bought it.

When she left, Grandpa returned immediately to the point.

"Mikey, I hope you don't take this unkindly, but you don't have enough friends. That fellow that left you his business, he was about the only person you regularly hung out with. You've always been a loner, even when you were a little boy, but there are times when a man needs friends. Of course, I don't have any friends much either. No, that's not right. I've got lots of friends. Unfortunately they're practically all dead. But when I was your age there were half a dozen pals I could call on, and they would've come running with a checkbook in one hand and a loaded pistol in the other ready to help whichever way I needed them."

"I've got you and Buddy."

"Yeah, well he can't shoot and I can't fight. I used to could, and I could still get one good punch in, but let's face it, I couldn't go toe to toe with a young man. Not no more."

"All you've got to do is stay home and watch out for yourself. And maybe Buddy sometimes."

"The hell that's all I got to do! I don't need a permit from the state of Texas to keep a weapon at home. Sooner or later you're going to need someone to ride shotgun or watch your back. And I want your promise to call on me when that time comes."

"Speaking of Buddy," I said, drawing a folded sheet of paper out of my pocket, "here's one of those tricky questions I got out of a puzzle book. It says a man living at the bottom of a mountain left his house at noon and climbed a mountain. He got to the top at 7 o'clock. He spent the night on top of the mountain and at noon he started down the mountain. He got home at 2 o'clock that afternoon."

"So it took him seven hours to get up and two hours to get back down. I guess that's reasonable."

"Yeah. The question is, was there ever a point on the path that he was both coming and going at the same time on the clock?"

"Well, I'd have to think about that for awhile. What's the answer?"

"The answer is yes. That's what the book said. So I tried the question on Buddy."

"And?"

"He said yes, too. But then he added without any pause that I noticed . . ." I unfolded the paper to be sure I had it right. "Buddy said the clock time in question was 1:34 p.m. and the spot was seventy-eight per cent of the way down the mountain. That wasn't in the book, but Buddy was right. It took me a couple of pages of algebra to verify it."

"Well, you're smart. I would've had to climb the damn mountain to verify it. How can Buddy be so smart and yet so helpless?"

"I don't know, Grandpa. They say that genius is next to insanity, but I think genius is next to autism."

When we got back to the shooting course, everybody took the written part of the test, which was all multiple-choice. Then they took a few of us at a time into the soundproof firing range, watched us load our weapons, and told us we had ten seconds to get off five shots at a range of twenty-five feet.

The target was a man silhouette with different zones marked out. The highest scoring zone took in a small circle in the center of the chest, another small circle in the center of the head, and a narrow strip connecting the two circles. The next highest scoring area was the rest of the head and neck and the central chest area. There were areas of descending score, the lowest being a hit just about anywhere within the silhouette. After two sets of five shots at twenty-five feet, there would be two sets at fifty feet and another two at seventy-five feet. Your total score had to come up to a certain number to qualify for the license.

Between sets the targets were oriented sideways, edge on. To start a set the targets would twist to present the silhouette. At the end of the allotted time they would abruptly twist back so you could see only the edge. If you hadn't gotten off all your rounds it was too bad.

I aimed for the head for the first two ranges, and for the center of the chest for the last one. I had no doubt that I had qualified.

When I came out, Grandpa was being shown into the range. He gave me a wink, and I gave him a thumbs-up. The bulk of his old autoloader seemed to diminish his small size, and I wondered how long it had been since he had fired that weapon. He seemed a little subdued when he came out, and there was nothing to do but wait.

When the last of the students had come back from the range, the two instructors put the paper targets in a stack and started calculating the scores. While they were summing up my score I moved up to see how I'd done. All the holes were in the highest or next highest zone except one flyer—I knew I'd pulled it when I fired—that just clipped the silhouette's shoulder, almost in the white. Mine was the highest score so far and I got some congratulations from the other shooters.

When they got to Grandpa's target everyone moved up to get a better look, and there was a lot of talk. All of his shots, every one of them, had gone into a small circle in the center of the target's chest. But what made his target a conversation piece was the fact that those oversize slugs—almost a half-inch in diameter—had overlapped and had simply taken out all the paper within the group except for a couple of slivers dangling from the ragged edge of the group. The silhouette looked like it had been the donor for a heart transplant.

The burly range instructor said, "I guess the moral of this story is that pistol shooting is a skill that, once learned, is never forgotten."

"No," Grandpa said, "The moral is don't mess with the old guys."

Back in the pickup, I asked Grandpa, "Did you remember to use both hands?"

"I didn't at first," he said. "I was half through before I remembered. So then I shot the rest with my left hand."

Grandpa is good at deadpan, so I wasn't sure he was pulling my leg.

CHAPTER 13
A PAIR OF JACKS

The day after Van Moot's threatening phone call, I called Jack Hinton in for a conference.

"Can it wait for about thirty minutes?"

"No hurry," I said, "Let's set it for straight up ten o'clock."

"Fine. I'll see you then."

I filled in the time by taking a pad of paper and sketching out the management scheme at DataDigm. I started with a box at the top of the page, and wrote my name, Michael Kidd, in that box. Then I drew two lines down to two more boxes sharing the same level and wrote John Hinton in one box and under his name, *Industry*. In the other box I wrote John McKinney and *Military*. Both of these Johns were usually called "Jack." More lines would descend from each of those boxes.

I drew a small box off to the side of my box with a line attached to it. I labeled this box *Staff* and wrote in the names of Antoinette Black, Jim Martinez, and Carl Hindman. Those of the staff had more than one job. Antoinette was really sort of an executive secretary as well as receptionist; Jim Martinez was treasurer as well as our accountant, and our security man, Carl Hindman, was also in charge of personnel. There was hardly enough to keep him busy with both jobs. Except for a few changes in low-level jobs such as janitors, DataDigm hadn't hired or fired anyone in months. I supposed there might be security matters that he worked on directly with the government, but mine was the only current clearance issue that he was working on.

I didn't really yet know the lower management people, much less those without management responsibilities, the actual workers who kept the business going, but I determined to keep adding to my chart until I had everyone's name included. I knew that the total of all of us was seventy-two, and I set myself the task of learning to recognize everyone by name.

At exactly ten o'clock Jack Hinton made his appearance. He was a silver-haired man in his sixties, of a very fair complexion, apparently in good physical shape except for a bit of a pot belly in its early stages of development. I handed him Van Moot's business card.

"Jack, you head up the non-military contracts. Do you know this man?"

Hinton studied the card for a good while. "Never heard of him," he said at last.

"Jack, what's going on with these analyses for Van Moot's company?"

"What do you mean? They're all pretty much the same. They send us the data and we process it through our computer programs and send them the results in the form of graphs and charts."

"But the results don't tell them where the oil or ore is."

"No, but it makes it easier for their geologists to figure that out."

"Hasn't it ever occurred to you that they're paying us way too much for what they get? We wrote the computer program with their money. They own it. They could take it home and run the data through their own computers for a tenth of what they're paying us."

"Well, when you put it that way I'll have to admit that I have wondered why they don't do that. The computer program was actually delivered to them with the first report. They really don't need us at all. My guess is that they are an incredibly busy and prosperous concern and don't sweat paying extra for something they are too busy to fool with."

"Still, it seems a very odd sort of contractual arrangement."

"I guess so. But it's really no different for the other exploration companies we do work for, both oil and mineral. The first analysis included the computer modeling that was used for all the subsequent work."

"How many other companies are you talking about?"

"Seven, twelve if you count the oil companies along with the solid ore people. And one of them we worked for before Van Moot's company."

"Jack, please send me copies of all the seismic reports."

About an hour after Hinton left his secretary showed up with an arm full of reports bound in slick DataDigm covers. Sure enough, it was the same deal with all of them. One legitimate initial analysis followed by a string of overpriced follow-ups. And only the very first of all the analyses required extensive original computer coding; all the rest were patterned after that one. *My God, Vince, what have you been up to?*

* * *

When my SECRET clearance finally came in Carl, our security man, took another photo of me and issued me a new badge. With it I could now go without escort into the part of the building in which the government contract work was conducted. So I boldly walked through the door marked SECURE AREA – VISITORS REQUIRE ESCORT without anyone accompanying me. The atmosphere in this part of the building was much more business-like than in the unclassified area. It was no sweat shop, but the workers here seemed to have more purpose in their actions and also in their conversations. The programmers that had modeled the seismic work were now employed here, and they were constantly modeling new things. As I was soon to learn, in the unclassified part of the building lesser qualified mathematicians ran new batches of unclassified data through the programs originated by these people.

Although the department head, Jack McKinney, had one of the big offices up front. I found him in one of the cubicle style offices in the secure area. He was a small man with close-cropped, dark brown hair that looked like it wanted to wave if allowed to grow a little longer. When I found him he was in earnest conversation with one of his subordinates. He nodded at me and I remained standing while he explained what his man was to do next.

"Is this a good time to talk?" I said as the man left.

"As good as any." He motioned me to sit down. "What's on your mind?"

"Now that I've got the proper clearance, I'd like to look over some of the reports you fellows put out. Do you do anything like the statistical analyses they put out in the other department?"

"We do serious work in this department. Our folks call the other department 'Der Goofenoffen Groupen.' The people that did their original modeling were good and hard workers. In fact they do most of their work over here now. But the ones over there now just do the same old thing over and over. If they have any really creative people over there now, they must be bored as hell."

I was surprised, but pleased, with his frankness. "Which group came first?"

"Ours did by about two years. We started with an idea Vince had about a laser locater. Not the laser that lights up a target for airplanes or artillery; that's a laser designator. The laser locater is a countermeasure to the laser designator. It locates the poor enemy guy using the designator and gives his coordinates to our artillery. It puts him out of business.

"Vince's idea was just theoretical. It had not been demonstrated. We asked the army for money to build and test a prototype. They liked the idea and we set up our own laser lab—why don't I show it to you?"

I followed him down a hallway to a door locked with a combination, which he worked and let us in. I had never been here before. There was no one in the lab, but the equipment was impressive. He pointed out several lasers of different power and wave length. The next thirty minutes were devoted to his explanation of various laser-related contracts they had done. He seemed quite proud of what they had accomplished. Finally he wound down and we started to leave.

"Wait a minute," he said. "Did Vince by chance refer to you as 'Buddy'?"

"That's my brother. Vince knew him well."

"Then I'd better give this to you," he said. He crossed the lab and picked up a box from the top of a table. He brought it back and handed it to me. "Ever since Vince died I've been trying to find out who this is for."

It was a plain cardboard box. On the top was written, "To Buddy from Vince."

CHAPTER 14
ASSEMBLING THE PIECES

I already knew what was in the package marked "For Buddy." The one activity that Vince and Buddy used to share was solving jigsaw puzzles. That fact plus the sound I heard when I shook the box left little doubt as to its contents.

"This is a gift to you from Vince," I said as I handed the package to him.

Ah, Vince, you and your games and puzzles. The fierce competitiveness that seemed to drive Vince would vanish when he and Buddy worked together on a jigsaw puzzle, and what would have been a contest if I had worked with him became a smooth work of cooperation with Buddy.

I think that was due to the fact that Buddy was better at it than Vince, so much better that Vince had no hope of beating Buddy or ever acquiring the skill necessary to match him. That fact put Vince into a quiet mood in which he acted more as an assistant to Buddy than as a competitor. Vince would build a section of the puzzle until Buddy saw where Vince's part would fit into the much bigger section he was building. Then Buddy would just stop and wait for Vince to realize he was waiting to unite the two sections. Then Vince would start assembling another section. Sometimes Vince would stop working and just observe Buddy, I suppose trying to figure out Buddy's method. It had always been a pleasure for me to watch the two of them.

"There's no picture on the box," Buddy said that night when I handed it to him.

Sure enough, the box was plain white on all sides. Buddy opened it and stared at the contents for about a full minute. Then he poured the pieces out on the kitchen table and began turning the colored sides up.

"This is going to be a hard one," he said.

"There must be a thousand pieces there," I said after Buddy dumped the contents out on the kitchen table.

"Almost two thousand. This is going to be a hard one."

I wasn't surprised because over time Vince had brought in larger and larger puzzles, many with tricky pictures designed to challenge the addicts.

"You can do it, Buddy."

"Yes. There are no edges. It's going to be a hard one."

I moved in close. He was right; there were no pieces with straight edges. Assembling the border is the easiest way to start on a jigsaw puzzle, but there would be no border here. The pieces were very small and looked almost identical. The pattern looked the same on all of them, too, dots and blotches of color suggesting that the completed image might be an example of abstract expressionism.

Well, Vince wouldn't have given it to Buddy if he didn't think he could work it, but I had to agree with Buddy. This was going to be a hard one. Buddy sat down and continued turning the pieces right side up. He didn't seem to be in a hurry. Maybe he was a little bit intimidated by the task.

I turned my attention toward Vanessa. She was wandering around as one does in a strange house, looking vaguely at different items, probably trying to tie what she saw with what she already knew about me. Or thought she knew. I wondered how she was reacting to Buddy. I told myself I didn't care, but I knew I did. Vanessa hadn't shown any of the characteristics of people who have strong aversions toward the mentally impaired, although that's not quite the right expression for Buddy. His mind is impaired in some ways but extraordinarily enhanced in other ways.

I would have been married by now if it weren't for my commitment to Buddy. The only woman I had asked to marry had forced me to choose between herself and Buddy. I told her that Buddy and I were a package and always would be. She told me that she loved me but living with Buddy in the house would depress her beyond her ability to bear it. And so we parted. At first I hated her for it, and then I began to hate Buddy.

Finally I realized that there was no one to blame but myself. It was in my power to rid myself of Buddy by having him committed. All the choices had been mine, were still mine to make. But putting Buddy away would ruin my chances of ever feeling happy, and if that meant never marrying, so be it. So why did I care what Vanessa thought one way or the other? *There's really nothing special about you, Vanessa.* But somehow there was.

"Very masculine," she said.

"What's that?"

"The décor in this house. It's about what you would expect. Two men and no women. Solid colors, no patterns. Lots of browns, nothing pastel. Hunting, fishing, and western motif. At least it's all neat and clean. Do you have someone come in to clean?"

"No, we do that ourselves. When we think of it."

She sat down on the couch and pointed to the vacant spot on the couch.

"Come sit down and let's go over what we have."

"Okay," I said, sitting down but not so close as to distract me from the business at hand. "This is about the way I see things. Somehow Vince learned something about Van Moot's operations to get an open-ended contract to do useless, or near useless, work—or really to pretend to do work—for year after year."

"No. That sounds like blackmail, and Vince wouldn't engage in blackmail."

"Maybe not blackmail, but something, some process, that would put Van Moot ahead of his competition. Something Vince came up with, owned, but he agreed not to sell to anyone on the condition of getting these make-believe analysis jobs."

"Then why not a lump sum, a one-time payment and that's that?"

"I don't know," I said. "Maybe for tax reasons. Maybe Van Moot wanted it that way—easier for him to pay off over time. Anyway, the secret process or formula or whatever has been released after Vince died. So somebody beside Vince knew about it. But Van Moot thinks I'm the one who let it leak. At least, he holds me responsible."

"And you think the person who released the secret is an employee at DataDigm?"

"That seems like the best bet. The secret process or whatever must have been what Vince had me burn. He kept his end of the bargain. He always did. That's the way he was."

We tossed ideas around for the next thirty minutes, without getting any further toward an answer. Finally Vanessa said, "We're not getting anywhere. How can we? We are desperately looking for something but we don't even know what it is."

"Captain Kidd's buried treasure," Buddy said.

He had come in from the kitchen and was standing behind us. He turned and walked back into the kitchen. We followed him to the table where the jigsaw puzzle lay, completely put together. Evidently Vince had bought a 2,000 piece puzzle, assembled it and painted over the original picture randomly with spray paints of various colors. He had then written a message across it with a felt marker, removed all the edge pieces, taken it apart, and put it in a box for Buddy. The message across the face of the puzzle was in cursive longhand. It said, "Captain Kidd's buried treasure."

Vanessa and I looked at each other, and then we looked at Buddy.

"It was a hard one," Buddy said.

CHAPTER 15
OLD FART

Vanessa's social life was beginning to broaden, and she was attending a book club dinner. So Buddy and I met Grandpa at the Turnip Patch for dinner, or supper as Grandpa calls it. You can tell by the name that the restaurant specializes in Southern country style cooking, not my favorite or Buddy's either, but it was Grandpa's, and Buddy and I can always find something we like. So we had chicken fried steaks while Grandpa indulged in pork chops, collard greens, black-eyed peas, and hot water cornbread.

Buddy's favorite restaurant is Whataburger, any of the half dozen in town, and his favorite dish is a small hamburger and large fries. Buddy's table manners are good despite his imperfect muscular coordination. And they should be. I'd spent endless hours teaching him to chew with his mouth closed and follow other conventions that he could see no sense in. Teaching him to cut up a steak with a knife and fork had been a challenge, and I had given up on getting him to cut and eat one piece at a time. If we had been in a hurry I would have cut the steak up for him. This time I let him cut up the steak into bite-sized pieces and then put down the knife and use only the fork on one piece at a time.

A chicken fried steak is a thin round steak battered and fried like chicken and served with white gravy. Sometimes it is sold as "country fried steak" but that usually means a lighter batter and brown gravy. They say the chicken fried steak started in Texas during the cattle drives when German-American cooks tried to make *vienerschnitzel*.

Grandpa and I both finished our meals before Buddy had gotten half way through his steak, so we took up the discussion of the mysterious briefcase again. I was speaking in a low tone to keep others from hearing when I noticed that Grandpa was leaning toward me when I talked. I looked at his ears in vain for signs of his hearing aid. I don't know whether it was his age that had degraded his hearing or whether it was from a lifetime of banging away at ducks, quail, and doves with shotguns in the field without ear protection. I guess it was a combination of both age and abuse.

I raised my voice a notch. "Forget your hearing aids?"

"Naw, I just don't like to wear them all the time. They make my shoes squeak."

It took me a second to get it. When he saw I did he laughed. "I wear them whenever I leave the farm. But they are worthless in restaurants. All those dishes clattering and people jabbering come in clearer than what I'm trying to hear. I'll put them on again when it's time to leave."

Grandpa had gotten there first, so I didn't realize he was using a walking stick until we had finished our meal and were out on the sidewalk.

"Since when have you been using a cane?" I said.

"Since about the same time I applied for that concealed carry permit," Grandpa said. "It'll take a few weeks for that permit to be processed. I'm not famous for following the letter of the law and I figure passing the test was almost as good as having the license, but I am patiently waiting for the license to come in. Meantime, I thought a stick might be a nice thing to carry while I'm waiting."

Stick was a better description than *cane*. The heavy walking stick he had with him looked sturdy enough to crack someone's back.

"In fact," Grandpa continued, "the thing about this stick is you don't have to conceal it and you don't have to drag it up out of a holster. It's right there in your hand to start with. And it don't look unusual for an old timer like me to be carrying it, neither."

I wanted to thank him for his concern over my problems but I knew it would just embarrass him if I did. Buddy seemed to be paying attention to what Grandpa was saying but it's always hard to tell how much he understood. Sometimes, days or weeks later he will repeat something of no consequence word for word.

Buddy is the slowest walker of the three of us and he was setting our pace, so we were moving pretty slowly when a car stopped in the street and three men got out leaving the driver in place. Almost running, they separated before they reached the curb so that one came up in front of us while the other two swung in behind us.

"Mr. Kidd," the man in front said, "we'd like a word with you. Would you mind stepping over to the car?"

We had to stop or run into him. I studied him. His face had some small fighting scars and he was muscular. His left arm didn't hang straight down but was toward the outside by about an inch, suggesting that he was wearing a shoulder holster under his coat. I glanced at their car but couldn't get a clear look at the driver's face.

"I don't think I want to do that," I said.

"Sure you do."

One of the men behind me touched me gently on the elbow, giving me a slight nudge. Grandpa took Buddy by the arm and started walking him forward and away.

"Come on, Buddy," he said, "This is none of our affair."

Grandpa's words surprised me, and when I looked at him I was still more surprised. He had shrunk and he was bent over. His steps were very small and he limped as he leaned heavily on his walking stick. For the first time he actually looked his age or even older. One of the two behind us came forward into my field of view and reached out toward Grandpa.

"Never mind the old fart and the dummy," the man in front said.

By this time Grandpa had moved slightly behind and to the side of the man doing the talking. The walking stick flashed out like a bat in the hands of a major leaguer and caught him across the back of both knees. As he buckled I grabbed the hand that was on my elbow and yanked the arm straight, at the same time twisting my body and applying pressure on *his* elbow with mine. He went down on his face, and I turned toward the third man. He was stepping toward me while drawing a pistol from under his coat. I saw the curved handle of Grandpa's cane snake around his ankle and jerk him off balance. As he fell toward me I used an uppercut to catch his jaw on the heel of my hand and I knew he was out of the fight.

The man who had done the talking was on his knees from the effect of Grandpa's stick on the back of his legs, so his face was in ideal position for the kick I delivered. The nudger was back on his feet but nursing a dislocated elbow as he ran for the car. The two men that were left were lying helpless. I took a pistol from each of them and handed one to Grandpa as we walked away.

We heard a groan followed by some profanity. The man I had kicked was tough, all right. He was sitting up and collecting himself. Grandpa quickly returned and laid him out properly with his cudgel.

"Who's a old fart, now?" he said.

"Who's a dummy?" Buddy said.

Grandpa and I were both holding pistols when I looked back at the car. The driver was just sitting there and the other fellow was in the car nursing his elbow. Grandpa had returned to his original size and shape and his eyes glittered with excitement. I didn't know what to expect in the future, but it was plain that this ruckus had made his day.

"Thanks, Mikey," he said, inspecting the .40 caliber auto I had just handed him. "By God, I'm going to start carrying this very pistol. It's small enough to hide and it has just acquired sentimental value. And I'm not going to wait for that concealed carry license, neither. If some busybody asks to see my license I'll, by God, just hand him a copy of the Second Amendment."

CHAPTER 16
CAPTAIN KIDD

About a week after our encounter with the armed men, I sat at Vince's office desk—I was beginning to think of it as *my* office and desk—and mulled over the riddle. It was dark outside and almost everyone had left for home.

Like Grandpa, I had decided to go around armed despite the fact that my concealed carry permit had not yet come through. I didn't carry a weapon inside DataDigm because of some rule I didn't understand about firearms on the premises where federal government work was done. So, I left my weapon in the car whenever I entered the building. After the run-in with the thugs I knew that next time would be harder, probably impossible, to survive without firearms. They may not encounter people who will resist very often. Now they knew what kind of people they were dealing with. I hoped that, since we hadn't been armed before, they would think that we would remain that way.

Of course, I didn't really know what their intentions were. Had I meekly walked over to the car with them that night they might have merely given me some kind of warning—or slapped me around—and let me go. But I had no regrets or even second thoughts about what Grandpa and I did. Once I got to the car they might have forced me in and driven off with me. And that could have been the last anyone ever saw of me.

I wasn't resisting for the fun of it; if I knew how to give Van Moot what he wanted, I would do it. It would have helped to know what it was that he wanted but he had danced around that issue. My concerns now were figuring out who had betrayed Vince (if anyone had) and how to keep Vanessa, Buddy, and Grandpa from getting hurt.

I had moved Buddy out to Grandpa's and checked by phone several times a day to see if they were all right. My greater concern right now was for Vanessa. I felt that I needed to be near her all the time to protect her, but at the same time I felt the more I associated with her the greater danger I placed her in. So I told her that I would check on her by cell phone but would not be dating her again until this situation clarified. She wasn't having any of that, and kept popping in at my house or Grandpa's. At least we weren't being seen together in public, and I was staying away from her home, Vince's old house.

Captain Kidd's buried treasure. The message from Buddy's jigsaw puzzle kept running through my mind. I could just imagine Vince enjoying his final game. He was challenging me to figure out a brainteaser. *If you've got something to tell me, Vince, damn it, just tell me.* But that was Vince, he loved puzzles and games, and he was challenging me.

I couldn't believe that he would have put my life in jeopardy over a game, so he hadn't known that someone else was involved. He had thought of a game between two players, Vince and Mike, but there were at least three not counting the rent-a-thugs. There was a third player, unseen and playing by unknown rules. I didn't mean Van Moot. He was possibly dangerous, but someone else had moved Van Moot into action.

Captain Kidd's buried treasure. Well, Captain Kidd had to be me; Mike Kidd, the name *Kidd* couldn't just be a coincidence. Thinking about it made me wonder if I was descended from the pirate. I had never heard any family history along those lines, in fact, I had never had much contact with my father's family, and I had little interest in genealogy. At any rate, if it was *my* buried treasure, that would mean I must have it in my possession. And that would indicate that it was somewhere at DataDigm.

DataDigm was not a large business, fewer than one hundred employees housed in a few thousand feet of offices, workshops, and laboratories. I had memorized all the door combinations and could now go almost anywhere in the building by myself. There were a few padlocked filing cabinets, safes, and a couple of rooms for which I still was not allowed the combinations because of what our security man Carl called "need to know," but Vince would have taken that into account and so would not have hidden something for me there. In fact, he couldn't have because he lacked the same "need to know" as I did; only those actually doing the government contract work had access.

I had spent several nights going all over the premises. I suspected that I was looking for a document of some kind, perhaps a statement by Vince clarifying everything. But was the document paper or digital? Between spells of roaming the labs and offices I was gradually going through every document on Vince's two office computers, one a desktop and the other a laptop. There were thousands of files but I was taking at least a cursory look at everything Vince had generated with a word processor. Searches for key words, notably "Captain Kidd" and "treasure" had yielded nothing. I was tempted to take the laptop home and search it there, but I figured the fact that DataDigm did classified government work would make anyone reluctant to break in for fear of the FBI, so I kept it in my office.

I looked at Vince's Monopoly clock and it told me that it was after eight, and that made me realize I was one meal short of the usual three. It's funny how looking at the clock will make a person hungry, at least it often had that effect on me. I thought of taking Vanessa out for dinner, but she probably would have eaten by now. Besides that was against the rules that I had laid down to avoid dragging her further into the mess. As I was thinking this my cell phone rang.

"Thank God you're there!" It was Vanessa's voice. "Mike I'm scared. There's somebody in my house."

"Then you get out! Keep your phone on and get out of the house. Now!"

"I'm already out. I'm standing outside, a couple of houses away. I was coming home and before I got to the front door I heard noises coming from inside the house. Should I call the police?"

"Yes, but don't tell them about anything except that someone is in the house. I'm on my way."

As I got within a few houses of Vince's place I slowed down. Vanessa appeared from the shadows on my right, and I pulled over and turned out the lights. It took only an instant to fetch the 9 mm semi-automatic from under the seat. It was in an inside-the-waistband holster, and as I got out of the car I crammed the holster and all inside my trousers just behind the right hip, and checked that the holster clip was locked on my belt. The pistol was a Turkish knock-off of a Berretta and I knew from putting several hundred rounds through it that it was reliable.

"The police not here yet?" I asked Vanessa.

"Not yet."

I cautioned Vanessa to stay by the car and I headed toward the house. The police should have beaten me to the scene since I had to drive from the outskirts. I had the pistol in my hand as I crossed the lawn silently and furtively in a half-crouch. I hesitated at the front door and listened. Silence. I tried the door. It was locked. I took the key Vince had given me from my pocket and slowly worked the lock. Then I pushed the door open with my foot and slipped inside.

I stopped and listened again to the silence. I moved from the foyer into the living room, swinging my weapon from side to side using the two-handed grip that Grandpa had disdained. There were no lights at all in the house and I could see very little. As I stepped back into the foyer, I switched on the living room lights. The room was empty, but disheveled. The cushions were out of the sofa and on the floor. A table drawer was upside down on the floor and its contents scattered.

As I entered the family room I heard the police siren. I switched on the light, and it revealed another tossing. There was a fica tree overturned but still in its pot near a corner. I righted the tree and pushed it into the corner. Then I slipped my pistol behind the tree pot. I started back out of the house, but as I reached the open front door a flashlight beam hit my eyes and a voice yelled, "Stop! Don't move!"

Without being told, I raised my hands over my head and wiggled my fingers to show they were empty. I heard Vanessa call from the yard, "That's my friend!" But the police weren't taking any chances. They had me in cuffs and patted down before I could say anything. There were two policemen, one a young crew-cut blond man, thin for a cop, the other a little older and both heavier and darker, possibly Hispanic, his black hair perhaps a little longer than regulation. He seemed to be the senior officer. The blonde stayed with me while the other proceeded to search the house. He didn't find anyone. After about ten minutes they let Vanessa in and she again identified me as not a burglar.

The young policeman seemed sorry to have to release me. As he took the cuffs off the older officer said, "That's pretty dumb, going into a house like that unarmed. Why didn't you wait for us? You knew we'd been called."

"Pure, blind stupidity of my part. I'm sorry."

The blonde was the one who had patted me down. He said, "I'm not so sure he was unarmed. He's got an empty concealed carry holster on him."

The dark officer looked at me. "Do you have a concealed carry permit?"

"I didn't know I needed one to carry an empty holster."

He looked at me for a few seconds and then smiled and turned to Vanessa.

"We don't know if they left before your friend got here or if he scared them away, but the house is empty now. The back door has been forced, and they evidently left the same way. Have you noticed anything missing?"

"No," she said. "But I'd have to check. I've only lived here a few weeks. It's my brother's house. Or it was until he died three month ago. They could have taken something of his and I might not know it."

Both officers took out notebooks and proceeded to ask us a set list of questions and to write down the answers. When I told them the front door was locked but I had a key, they exchanged knowing glances. Finally, they asked Vanessa to go over the house tomorrow and report anything missing.

After they left, I retrieved my pistol and put it back into the holster. I should have hidden the holster with it, but you can't think of everything. Then I inspected the back door. Entry had been obtained by the common method of kicking the door hard enough to break the striker plate out of the door jam. Most house burglaries are accomplished by this means. I closed the door and took a chair from the breakfast room to brace the door closed with the chair back wedged under the doorknob and the back legs on the floor. It was now more secure than it had been when relying on the lock, but that still wasn't good enough to reassure me, and I knew it wouldn't satisfy Vanessa.

I looked at her. She was bearing up pretty well, but she had that dazed look that goes with any kind of narrow escape. I figured she was thinking about what would have happened if she had blundered into the house while the criminals were still there. I walked over to her and put my arms around her. After a few seconds she hugged me back. I half expected her to start crying, but she didn't. I released her from my embrace but took her hands.

"Okay," I said. "You're not staying alone in this house tonight. Do you want me to stay here or do you want to come home with me? Or do you want me to find a room for you in a hotel?"

"I want you to stay here."

CHAPTER 17
LONG JOHN SPILLS HIS GUTS

As the excitement from the burglary wore off I began to feel hungry. Vanessa had already eaten so she made coffee and sipped on it while I raided her refrigerator. Soon I was sitting across from her munching on a bologna and provolone sandwich with potato chips on the side and drinking iced tea. We had reached that comfortable condition in our relationship in which silences were no longer embarrassing, so we just smiled at each other until I had wiped the last crumb from my lips.

"Do you feel up to inspecting the damage?" I asked. "I'd like to see if the crooks left any clue as to what they were looking for. And if they didn't find it, maybe we can spot something they overlooked. You know, we haven't really looked through Vince's stuff here."

"I'm up to it. You know that some of the things in this house are yours. Vince left you the games."

That reminder jolted my interest. The games in this house—and there were lots of them—were my property, and I had concluded that what I was searching for would be contained in something belonging to me. *Captain Kidd's buried treasure.* I had completely forgotten that I owned property within Vince's house. There could be a message for me coded into any of the electronic games.

We started our inspection in the living room, partially cleaning up as we went. Vanessa did not notice anything missing as we progressed. The items from the overturned table drawer were mostly photographs and receipt slips of paper along with a motley group of paperclips, pencils, and other small items common to all households.

"I haven't used this drawer. All this is Vince's. I wouldn't know if something is missing," she said. She started to turn the drawer right side up, but I stopped her to inspect the bottom surface. There was nothing there so I turned it over so she could replace the spilled contents.

"I wanted to see if Vince had taped something to the drawer bottom," I said. Vanessa nodded and began replacing everything to the drawer. I ran my fingers down into the couch and chair crevices without finding anything but a couple of kernels of old popcorn. Then I pinched the sofa and chair cushions as I replaced them. Nothing.

We went next to the family room and started going through it in the same manner, finding nothing we could associate with the mystery. I wanted to be methodical and go through the house room by room, but I felt myself drawn to the game room. So, before we had really done justice to the family room, I said, "To hell with this. Let's go on to the game room."

"I was thinking the same thing, myself."

The burglars must have also thought the same thing because we found the game room to be a real mess. Vince had collected games of all sorts, from the sophisticated laser-driven interactive sports to old-fashioned, coin-operated pinball machines. He had several Japanese box-shaped games that customarily hung on the wall. These were lying on the floor, some of them broken. In fact, everything that had hung on the wall, including pictures and clocks had been removed and thrown onto the floor, leading me to think that the crooks had been looking for a wall safe.

The big pinball machines had been pulled away from the wall for the same apparent purpose. The pool table looked as if it hadn't been touched, but the poker table was upside down with its legs sticking up like a dead animal. I couldn't see any signs of tape residue, so evidently nothing had been stuck on the underside of the table. All furniture of whatever type with drawers now stood with the drawer slots agape like open mouths as if they hadn't got over the shock of being robbed. The drawers lay empty on the floor, their contents scattered.

"The laptop is gone," Vanessa said.

"The laptop? Vince's laptop computer?"

"It belonged to you, remember? Along with the games you got whatever electronic devices were in the house, including computers?"

"Was there another one?"

Vanessa disappeared into the bedroom. She was back within a few seconds. "Yes, there was a tablet-sized computer, but it's gone, too."

"Damn! I had forgotten all about that." I silently cursed myself for not removing them from the house weeks ago.

"He left you all the games, too. But I don't think any of them are missing."

"Yes, he did leave me all his games. I remember now." I started walking down the row of electronic games, studying them for some clue. Vince had set up separate screens for several games, although I knew that all the games could have used the same screen. A five-wheeled stenographer chair was nearby for conveniently moving from one game to another.

The most promising seemed to be an electric eye rifle that the player shot at the screen with. I had played this with Vince. The screen would light up with rabbits, ducks, deer, and a bear. The animals cavorted around the screen while the player shot at them and a running counter kept score. That was the sort of competitive thing Vince loved, and one of the few that I could consistently beat him at.

"Captain Kidd's Buried Treasure."

"What?" I looked around at Vanessa. She was standing in front of one of the vintage coin-operated pinball machines. The back panel showed a pirate scene and contained a legend proclaiming "Long John Silver's Treasure Hunt."

"Don't forget that these antiques are also yours," Vanessa said.

"But this says 'Long John Silver' not 'Captain Kidd,'" I said as I walked over to join her.

She pointed to the smaller printing on the panel. It was a list of rewards that high scores would get you. The rewards were numbers of free games. Each had a name and the number of points required along with the number of free games awarded. The levels were, in ascending order, Blackbeard's Pirate Chest, Captain Morgan's Sunken Jewels, Captain Blood's Cache, and *Captain Kidd's Buried Treasure.*

We looked at each other without speaking. Then I walked around the machine looking for a switch, a hidden door, anything unusual. I found nothing except a large button on each side and the electric power cord, which was plugged into a multiple outlet that fed several other pinball machines. I pressed the buttons one at a time and then simultaneously with no result. Next to the coin slot was the spring-loaded ball launcher, which I pulled with no effect.

I looked underneath the table part and saw a push button switch right under where you would ordinarily put in the quarters. Vince must have installed this to keep from having to keep a stack of quarters on hand to start every game. I pushed the switch and the pinball machine came to life. The upright panel lit up simultaneously with a musical flourish. Lights also came on and flashed on the playing surface. A "Your Score" sign showed up on the panel and displayed a row of zeroes. About a dozen steel balls sprang up and rolled down into a slot next to the launcher.

I pulled the plunger handle to compress the spring and a ball moved into the launching chute and nuzzled against the business end of the plunger. I released the handle and the ball sped up to the top of the playing field and began a descent slowed down by bumping into lighted posts along the way.

Then I remembered what the side buttons were for and began to use them to operate flippers that would help direct the ball into various scoring holes or bumpers in the playing field. When the ball landed in one of these holes it would stay there while a score was noisily rung up on the panel. Then it would shoot out of the hole and continue its descent down the sloping surface and disappear.

My score for this first ball was several hundred points although I didn't apply much in the way of skill. I used up the remaining steel balls, doing slightly better each time. Final score: 1,245 points. Then the score returned to all zeroes and the machine shut down.

"Keep at it," Vanessa said. "Push the switch again."

"The problem is that to reach the level "Captain Kidd's Buried Treasure" I need 500,000 points. After a month of practice I might be able to do it."

"There must be a shortcut."

I inspected the pinball machine again, but I didn't see how to get the glass cover off. Looking around the floor, I spotted a small throw rug. I brought it over to the machine and laid it over the glass. Then I fetched a 5-pound barbell from Vince's corner gym and brought it down sharply on the rug. I was lucky in that I had not overdone my blow. The glass was broken, but it had not shattered in a thousand pieces, nor had I damaged the playing surface. I began removing the glass shards so that the surface was exposed. Vanessa had by this time brought some damp paper towels from the kitchen, and she used them to pick up the smaller pieces that lay on the slope.

We didn't rush. We sensed we were in for an emotional climax of excitement or disappointment, and we needed a little time to prepare ourselves. We cleaned up and carried away the glass and dumped it in the trash, saying hardly a word to each other. Then we took our positions in front of the Long John Silvers Pirate Treasure pinball machine, and I pushed the starter button.

The machine again came to life, and a new group of steel balls came down to nuzzle one another next to the launcher. This time I picked up one of the balls and dropped it into one of the scoring holes. My score started rising. After a few seconds the ball shot out of the hole and I grabbed it and dropped it back. Again my score started climbing—50-75-100—then the ball jumped out again.

"Put it in this hole!" Vanessa said, pointing. "It scores more."

I dropped it where she indicated and my score climbed faster, a hundred points each ding the machine made while the ball was in the hole. By the time the ball popped out Vanessa had found the highest scoring hole and was pointing to it. I dropped it in and watched the score climb a thousand points a ding. When the ball jumped out I put it back and continued to ding up points. We watched as the score climbed. The ball would pop out, and I would just push it back in. As the score got over 100,000 points our anticipation and excitement grew with the numbers—200,000, 240,000, 300,000, 400,000, 490,000.

We passed all the other award levels, each time with a fanfare from the machine.

At 500,000 the top panel lighted up the words "Captain Kidd's Buried Treasure" with an extra prolonged fanfare. There was a simulated fireworks display. And then, the machine went dead.

I stared at the pinball machine for a good 20 seconds, and then I turned and looked at Vanessa. She was looking at me. "What next?" she said.

I walked around the machine again. Nothing had changed. Then I stooped down and looked up at the bottom. There was a change. A panel had released and dropped open on its hinges, exposing a rectangular opening.

I reached in and my fingers detected a string or cord. I gently pulled and dragged a velvet bag to the opening and let it drop into my other hand. It was soft and felt something like a two-pound bean bag. I stood up, showed it to Vanessa, and laid it down on the top surface of the pinball playing surface. I loosened the string and reached inside the bag to bring out a folded piece of paper. I set this down and reached back in and felt many small objects. They had edges and gave me the impression of small gambling dice. I could only get a small portion of the total in my hand, which I pulled out and opened. The objects reflected the lamps in dazzling points of light. Vanessa and I whispered in harmony, "Diamonds!"

CHAPTER 18
A VOICE FROM THE URN

"Diamonds!" we had said together. It was several seconds before either of us moved or spoke again. At last I carefully returned the gems to the bag. I noticed that my hand had begun to sweat so that a couple of the smaller jewels tried to cling to it. Making sure that all had been replaced, I wiped my hand on my trousers leg and opened the paper that I had taken from the bag. I went to one of the overturned poker chairs and turned it right side up for Vanessa. Then I got another one and set it beside the first.

"I think maybe we should sit down for this," I said.

"I think I need to."

I unfolded the paper. The message it contained had been generated with a word processor and printed by a computer printer. I read aloud.

> Congratulations Mike! I knew you could do it. I wish I could have seen your face when you found the diamonds. This is the story of how and why I give them to you.
>
> Not long after I started DataDigm I got a contract with the army that required a substrate of diamond in an electro-optical system. We used more or less standard

technology for forming a diamond film. That is, we evaporated carbon in a vacuum and let it coalesce as diamond. After completion of the contract work, I kept the apparatus to play around with, and came up with a brainstorm.

Small industrial diamonds have been manufactured for years. More recently, gem sized diamonds have been synthesized. These are available as jewelry and can be distinguished from natural diamonds only by the fact that they fluoresce under certain wavelengths of light whereas the natural ones don't. The diamond lobby has made sure that such gems must be engraved to announce that they are synthetic. They make just as beautiful jewelry and sell for much less than the natural ones, but still at a price above that of costume jewelry. What they lack is the emotional satisfaction that goes with knowing you have the romance and expense associated with natural diamonds.

Well, I conceived an idea to synthesize diamonds that would not fluoresce, and therefore be indistinguishable from the expensive naturals. While I was developing this idea I began to wonder how difficult it would be to take uncut diamonds to New York or Amsterdam and sell them. Then I got my second brainstorm. I would grow my diamonds already cut. I cannot, for ethical reasons, explain any part of the process. I sold that knowledge to the diamond cartel to be delivered after my death—my natural death. I'll just say that it involved vaporizing carbon in a vacuum chamber with a window transparent to a special wavelength laser beam, and rotating the chamber under computer control as the diamond grew.

I'm a good hand at computer programming and electronics, as you know, and have some skill in machining parts. But I required help from my employees. I parceled out the work and kept those working separated from one another and uninformed about what the others were doing as best I could in a small company. I succeeded in getting everything constructed without anyone being aware of what the final objective was.

What you see in this bag is the result of this experiment. These diamonds were produced with the same facets as are used by diamond cutters. There are various standard cuts and my program reproduces several of them, including some old fashioned ones that are no longer used. They are my farewell present to you. I hope I put you through enough head scratching, but I wanted one more game with you. Besides, I didn't want anybody else to chance upon these rocks. They are yours. We'll laugh about it together on the other side, but I hope that won't be for many years.

I found that I could easily sell them one at a time at any jewelry store that was locally owned. I sold several to pawn shops, but the jewelry stores offered a better price. I advise you not to sell a bunch at one time.

Well, old pal, that's how I made my first fortune. The DataDigm business was doing fairly well at the time, but my big bucks came from peddling homemade pre-cut diamonds. Then it occurred to me that more money could be made by selling my process to the diamond cartel. That's how I made my second fortune. I got in touch with some of the major diamond producers. It was a little hard getting their attention at first, but I finally met with a group of the big guys and showed them the very diamonds you now hold in your hands. That amounts to several million dollars even at wholesale, so they knew I wasn't pulling their legs. I also showed them videos of the diamonds being formed and how the growth would be stopped by the laser to create the proper facets. You could set the carat size and the cut you wanted and grow a large diamond in a few hours. They tested the stones by trying to make them fluoresce and a slough of other ways besides, some that I had never heard of. Finally, they were satisfied.

So we cut a deal. I could keep the diamonds I had already made—you're looking at most of them—but I would dismantle my device and not make any more. They would pay me a cash down payment and so many millions of dollars over the next so many years. I would deliver the plans for building my device at the end of the specified term. I would guarantee that no one would learn from me how to duplicate the process. I also told them that I had arranged things so that the whole process would be made public if I should die other than a natural death. I was going to have you do that but I am now almost sure to die a natural death, so don't worry about it.

They didn't seem as interested in the process as I had expected. For all I know they may already know how to do this. For all I know they may be selling their own synthesized diamonds and representing them as coming from their mines. When gem quality rubies were synthesized years ago, the hand writing was on the wall. When industrial diamonds were synthesized, the letters were boxcar size with floodlights on them. They spelled out, *Only a fool would invest in gemstones.'* At any rate, what they have been paying me for is to keep my process secret. It was their idea to give DataDigm lucrative contracts to analyze their data and make their agreed-upon payments in this way. I don't know why, other than taxes. It helped me in that regard, also. I got the money but also incurred tax deductable expenses. (I don't think you want to keep this document very long.) The contracts for seismic analysis are from different companies, but they are all owned or controlled by the cartel. They will stop within five years of my death, which will not be very long. Give the flash drive to Hendrik Van Moot; he is the diamond people's point man.

Do as you like, Mike. Run the business or sell the business and live off the diamonds. The main thing is, do what makes you happy. So long, pal.

It was signed by Vince.

We sat still for a couple of minutes. Then Vanessa said, "What flash drive?"

CHAPTER 19
DOWN BUT NOT OUT

It was a feeling that woke me up. Fear. It wasn't a panicky fear; it was more of a nagging feeling that something wasn't right and that I needed to get moving to make it right. But I didn't know why. My eyes seemed to be stuck shut as if I had been asleep for a long time dreaming bad dreams. Dreams about Vanessa needing my help and I couldn't get to her. Dreams about Gar Paine. And Benny the dealer saying, "Sure you have a diamond flush, everybody's got a diamond flush, all the up-cards are diamonds."

I couldn't make my eyes open. I tried to move my hand to my face to find out why. Then I discovered that I couldn't move my hand, either. That didn't bother me much. There was the soft droning nearby of people talking just above a whisper. I was lying on my back. I didn't clearly know where my hands were but thought they were more or less lying by my sides. Good. I was afraid that they might have been crossed on my chest and I had the starring role in a wake or viewing. I had been half expecting to hear someone say, "Doesn't he look natural."

Relax, I told myself. *Don't worry. Take it easy.* I tried to stop thinking. The voices buzzed on. I recognized them as belonging to Grandpa and

Vanessa. The feeling of fear gave way to a feeling of sleepiness. *They're all right. I'm all right. I just need to rest. I'm not really paralyzed. It's just sleep paralysis. I can't move because I'm not fully awake.* I couldn't figure out what was going on. The last thing I remembered was holding a fortune in diamonds in my hand. I began to listen. Grandpa was talking.

"Not so much lonely, as homesick," he was saying. "I feel like a tourist in a foreign country and the tour group has left without me. The America I knew is somewhere else, and I can't go home. I guess old people have always felt that way. But I look around and think, where am I? The men wear earrings and the women wear tattoos. I'm not saying that's wrong. You may have a beauty of a tattoo somewhere on your body, and that's your business. Things aren't wrong, just different. Like in a foreign country. Even the language is not the same. I need to adjust but I can't. I find myself in a country where women use words that men in my time wouldn't say in front of women. And I just want to go home, but I can't."

"Well," Vanessa said, "they say you can't go home again."

"Yeah, but that's for people who left the town they grew up in. If they go back they find the old place so changed that they hardly recognize it. In my case, I never left home. I was born in the same house I'm still living in. And yet, the world is so different that I'm out of place. Hell, you not only can't go home again, you can't even stay home."

"But back then, things hadn't changed that much, had they? They'd been the same for a long time."

"Times have always been changing, but they changed a lot slower in those days. No they hadn't changed much, at least not in East Texas. Not many had college degrees and most women didn't hold regular jobs. And people tended to stay married once they tied the knot."

"So it hit Mike pretty hard when his dad left?"

"Yeah, he was devastated sure enough. He thought the sun and the moon belonged to his daddy."

I didn't want him to tell Vanessa anything about my father and me. It ought to have made me mad to hear Grandpa tell her about that son-of-a-bitch, but I was too tired and sleepy to care much. I tried opening my eyes again. My eyelids felt as heavy as manhole covers, but they came open a crack and through a picket fence of eyelashes I could see the two of them near the foot of the bed. My eyelids were just too heavy so I let them close. From the brief glance I had made it looked like a hospital room, but I didn't remember being admitted to a hospital. What I remembered was a bag of diamonds. What happened to them? And what happened to me?

My mind came into focus just long enough for me to put two and two together and come up with a rough approximation of four. Somebody must have slugged me and stolen the diamonds. Then I lost focus and just lay there listening to Grandpa.

Grandpa is naturally talkative and he was filling Vanessa in on family history that I would rather have kept in the family. The funny thing is it didn't bother me as much as I would have expected. I know now that was because I had begun to look on Vanessa as family.

"The thing is," Grandpa said, "Vern wasn't a bad man even if he did a bad thing in running away from his family. I liked him. Everybody liked him. Caroline and me couldn't have asked for a better son-in-law. But that was only up until Buddy was born. The simple fact is that some people—mostly men, I guess—just can't abide being around the mentally crippled. Vern was one of those.

"He couldn't stand a lot of what other people don't much mind. He didn't want to be around when it was time for hog butchering, for instance. And he didn't want to visit sick folks. And he was sort of finicky about plates and dinnerware being really clean. He didn't mind work, though, and the getting dirty that comes along with it. He was an auto mechanic, and a good one. But he would clean up, take a shower and change clothes every day as soon as he came in from work. He read a lot, read more books than was good for him. Mikey got that from him, though he doesn't want to think he got anything from Vern. It was Vern that taught Mikey chess. And Mikey was a natural at it. Used to play against grown men in tournaments when he was just a kid. But that was after Vern left.

"What I'm getting at is that even though Vern had his peculiarities he was basically all right until Buddy came along. At first he seemed glad to have a second son but after a few months it became clear that Buddy wasn't going to be normal. Mattie—that's my daughter, now deceased—she began to notice how Vern was changing, and the more he changed the more she changed, too. The more Vern ignored Buddy, the more love she poured onto the little fellow. And it seemed like she only had so much love to give, so she started taking away from her store of love for Vern and transferring it onto Buddy. And from Mikey, too. He began to get the short end of the love stick, too.

"Sometimes Vern would act like Buddy didn't exist and would look every which way except where Buddy was. Other times I'd see him stare at Buddy for minutes at a time, reminding me of a scientist looking at a bug or a doctor at a sore trying to decide if it needed lancing. Vern started coming home late. I don't think he was playing around or even stopping for a drink at a bar. I saw him parked in his car one time just staring out the windshield. He just didn't want to go home and face Buddy. By that time Mattie was treating him almost like a stranger. They didn't try to talk things out. Maybe they could have at first, while they still loved each other, but it went too far for that so Vern just left.

"I thank God he did leave, because if he had stayed he would have killed Buddy. He wouldn't have planned it. It would have built up over time. He would have brooded over what a good life he had enjoyed up until what he thought of as a monster had come to take it all away. He couldn't see that he was doing it to himself. In his eyes Buddy was doing it. The disgust would have grown until he would have blown up one day all of a sudden and put an end to Buddy like you or I would squash a cockroach. That's why he left. I think he could see that in his future if he stayed."

"But that's horrible," Vanessa said, her voice raised to almost normal speaking volume. Then there was quiet for awhile. I guessed they were looking at me to see if was awake. I wanted to show them that I was, but just didn't seem to have the energy to make the effort. Besides, I was mulling over what Grandpa had said. It was all true, I thought. And hearing it that way from Grandpa made me think a little less harshly about my father. Maybe he wasn't any worse than a lot of men. Maybe he was just a miserable, flawed human being like most of us. Like myself.

Finally Grandpa said, his voice down to the almost whisper level, "It must not be all that rare, that feeling of disgust toward cripples. I've heard that the ancient Greeks and Romans used to kill babies that were deformed. And I think they weren't the only ones that did that, either. And part of it is just hating anything that's different, like hating somebody 'cause his skin is a different color or he talks with a funny accent.

"Anyhow, Vern just didn't come home from work one day. He never said goodbye or anything. He didn't even pack. All he took was that worn-out Ford sedan they had. He left everything else for Mattie. Of course, it wasn't much and Mattie didn't have a job. So Caroline and me, we helped out. My old farm kept us all fed pretty good so we got along all right. The funny thing is—what they call ironic—that Mattie kept the little farm she and Vern had and she got a job at the glove factory and made the payments on the mortgage. She just about had it paid for before she died. And here's the thing that's ironic. The oil people never found anything on my place, but they brought in a good well on Mattie's. Not a gusher, but a steady producer.

"Mattie never saw any of that money; it didn't start coming in until she was already dead. But she worked it so that it went to a trust for Mikey and Buddy to share equally. I was the trust manager and I never let the boys have but a smidgen until Mikey started college. Then I started doling it out, but I never let him have more than he would have made working at a regular job. Of course, he and Buddy get it all when I die. But it ain't that much; just about enough for the two of them to keep body and soul together. If Mikey wants to live good he'll always have to work some."

"You thought it would be bad for his character," Vanessa said, "to give it to him all at once?"

"That's part of the reason, all right. But mainly because that's the way the money comes into the trust from the oil company. Every six months a deposit is made automatically. I'm letting the trust fund build up gradually but there isn't one big pile that I could give to Mike. What he gets is Buddy's, too. He's Buddy's legal guardian and has his power of attorney "

"And Mike's father? Didn't he have some legal claim to the oil money?"

"That's why we're pretty sure he's dead. He had kin in the area and he would surely have heard about the oil. When Mattie died we were afraid he would show up to claim it, but he didn't. If he had there would have been some sort of legal hassle because it was Mattie that paid off the mortgage. Anyway, we had a lawyer make a search for him and he couldn't be found, so he was declared either dead or otherwise not entitled to the property, I forget the fancy legal terminology. It could be that he's alive and is just decent enough not to make a claim. I wouldn't be surprised.

"Anyway, Mikey sort of took his daddy's place as far as Buddy was concerned. And his mother's place, too, after she died. But after he got out of high school, I think he sort of got tired of watching out for Buddy. I sort of suspect that, just for a while, he began to feel a little bit of what his father had felt, a sort of disgust with Buddy. I'm no psychiatrist, but that's why I think Mikey hates Vern so much. You know, 'There but for the grace of God go I.' By hating Vern he keeps that part of himself under control."

I didn't want to think about that. I wanted to say, *You're wrong there, Grandpa*, but I couldn't rouse myself to make the effort. Then I heard Vanessa say, "You mean he overcompensated for a feeling he was ashamed of?"

"That's the word, *overcompensated*. While he was in school he got into a lot of fights over Buddy. No one could laugh or say anything disrespectful about Buddy without having to fight Mikey. I guess I had a hand in that, too, because I taught Mikey how to box. He cleaned all their plows, had a natural talent for fighting.

"Yeah, overcompensation for his own feelings is probably right. I think that's why he signed up for a hitch in the marines, so he could get away from Buddy for a few years. He was in some special forces sort of thing—he never explained it very well—but he came back with some fighting skills that not many men have. And he got closer to Buddy than ever, treating him more like the brother he is and not so much like a son."

I was half asleep, but I took in all of what Grandpa said. I wanted to argue with him while he was speaking, but as I lay there mulling it over I began to think that I should have talked this out with Grandpa a long time ago. I felt myself sinking into a comfortable sleep but then I suddenly remembered. Vanessa and I had the diamonds and we were reading Vince's letter, "Give the flash drive to Hendrik Van Moot; he's the diamond people's point man."

Then Vanessa said, "What flash drive?"

Yeah, I remembered.

CHAPTER 20
INSOMNIA

Vanessa and I stood in Vince's house looking at each other. I knew what a flash drive was; a handy portable data storage device, about the size of a small pocket knife, that can be plugged into any computer, loaded with data, unplugged and carried to another computer. I ran my hand back into the velvet bag. I felt the diamonds, still exciting to the touch, and ran my fingers all around the bag's interior twice before I felt something else. It was a small roll of paper. I pulled it out and handed it to Vanessa, and she unrolled it. It appeared to be regular printer paper cut down to about the size of a business card. It was blank except for one hand lettered word—"GAR."

"That could be a word or initials, G.A.R.," Vanessa said. "Does it mean anything to you?"

"Yeah. It means Vince wasn't putting all his eggs in one basket. There was one other person that Vince evidently trusted to deliver the goods to Van Moot if I failed."

"Somebody whose initials are G.A.R.?"

"No, somebody whose name is Gar, Gar Paine."

"And you know him?"

"He runs a high-stake poker game in Houston. I've played poker there with Vince. If the game is still in the same place, I know how to get there."

"I never heard Vince mention him. Was he a good friend of Vince?"

"He must have been. At least he thought enough of Vince to come up from Houston to attend his memorial service."

"Don't tell me he was that little man who raved about Vince being the world's best poker player."

"No. But he was there. The excitable little man works for him. He's one of Gar's dealers."

We went back into the family room and talked for a couple of hours. Among other things, we planned a trip to Houston for the next day. Finally Vanessa got up.

"I don't know about you, but I'm heading for bed. This excitement has just about worn me out."

"You go ahead. I'm going to stay up until daybreak. I don't want to take a chance on those crooks coming back and catching us asleep."

She walked toward the master bedroom but turned before she went out. "Well," she said, "there are four bedrooms and all the sheets are clean. When you finally give up you can sleep in any of the bedrooms you like."

She had my attention. "Let's see," I said. "There are four bedrooms, including the one you'll be in, and I can sleep in any of the four I choose. Is that right?"

"Damn!" she said as she walked out. "You really are good at breaking codes and figuring out puzzles."

Like a fool I did sit up, alternately fingering the bag of diamonds and my Turkish Berretta semi-automatic pistol, but thinking mostly about Vanessa. Vanessa taking her clothes off, Vanessa in the shower, Vanessa putting on a see-through black negligee, Vanessa lying in bed. Although I felt a little tired, I wasn't sleepy.

When I saw the first glow of dawn hit the windows, I went into one of the guest bedroom bathrooms and took a shower while the velvet bag and the pistol rested on top of the toilette tank.

I dried off and, leaving my clothes hanging on the door hooks and the wet towel over the shower door, I picked up the bag and the pistol and went down the hall to Vanessa's room. The door was open. She was lying there on her side, the bed covers pulled down to the footboard. She was wearing a sheer lavender nightgown that was somehow even more provocative than the black one I had imagined. Her eyes were open and she smiled as she looked me over.

I came to the bed and shoved the diamond bag and the pistol under the pillow she wasn't using and lay down beside her and rolled onto my side to face her. We lay there, not touching, looking at each other in the half-light.

Her dark hair contrasted with the white pillow and framed her face. Her large dark eyes seemed to glow. The lavender nightgown revealed as much as it hid. Her nipples were visible through the sheer fabric, and a dark area suggested her pubes. I reached out and lay my hand softly on her shoulder, then let it follow the contour down her side to her waist and then up to her hip. I rested it there and enjoyed the sensuous feel of her skin through the diaphanous cloth.

"I've been awake all the time," she said. "I thought the dawn would never break."

Together we gently removed the nightgown as one might remove expensive wrapping paper from a still more precious gift.

CHAPTER 21
BAIT FISH

Vanessa and I both slept until almost noon. She found Vince's electric shaver for me and also some of his underclothes and a clean shirt and socks. I couldn't find a packaged toothbrush in any of the bathroom drawers. A couple of Vince's used ones stood in a ceramic holder. Vince hadn't died of anything contagious and I figured it would be safe to use one of the brushes. But I couldn't bring myself to do it so I brushed, or rather, cleaned my teeth with my finger tip loaded with toothpaste.

As I was performing this awkward task I vowed to start carrying an overnight bag in the pickup. When I finished dressing all I was wearing from yesterday were my trousers and shoes. The shirtsleeves were a little long, but not enough to be noticeable, especially after I put on my jacket.

I was afraid that Vanessa's land line might be bugged, so I used my cell to call Grandpa. He and Buddy were both fine. I told him that Vanessa and I would be going to Houston and probably not be back until tomorrow. He didn't ask any questions. I guess he was thinking about tapped phones, too. Then I called the office and told

Antoinette that I wouldn't be in today and probably tomorrow as well.

It's about a four hour drive to Houston, five hours if you get there during the morning or afternoon commuter traffic. I couldn't find a phone listing for Gar Paine but I knew I could find his game again if it hadn't moved. It was in a swanky apartment in a high rise almost downtown. There was no point in getting there before Paine, and that should be not long before the dealing started, which meant about eight o'clock. So we had a few hours to kill before leaving.

Just off the garage Vince had a large shop equipped with both wood- and metal-working machines. I rummaged around in the scrap box and found enough steel pieces to rig up a crude, temporary secure lock for the back door. While I was installing this, Vanessa called a home security business and made appointments to install monitored systems in her house, my house, and Grandpa's house.

"You know what?" she said. "It's nice to be rich. I realized after I hung up that I hadn't even thought to ask the price."

"What I can't figure out is why Vince didn't already have an alarm system. What if somebody had broken in and stolen that pinball machine?"

"I guess he figured nobody would take it when there were so many other more valuable items in the house."

"Yeah, and maybe he thought that if he lost them he could just make some more. Well, I'm not going to wag a fortune of diamonds around with me. The first thing we're going to do when we leave the house is to put them in a bank safety deposit box."

"Do you have one?"

"No, but it shouldn't take but a few minutes to get one. I think they just add a fee to your bank statement. Like you say, it's nice not to care about the cost of things."

I took the diamond bag into the kitchen and weighed it. My guess had been two pounds. That was based on years of estimating the weight of fresh caught black bass I had taken from the many lakes of East Texas. I would guess their weight before actually weighing them. Then I would return them to the water. There is a natural tendency to over estimate the weight of fish that I had overcome by this practice, finally getting to be accurate to within an ounce or so. The kitchen scale verified my estimate, just a tiny tad over two pounds.

And indeed it took only a few minutes to make the transaction at the bank. Alone in a little alcove, I took the velvet bag out of my jacket pocket. Before putting it into the box I couldn't resist pouring some of the gems out into my hand and inspecting them again. The excitement returned in an instant.

Synthetic though I knew them to be, they still were valuable, especially if Vince was right about their being indistinguishable from the natural stones even by experts. I wanted to test that concept, even though I had a great deal of faith in Vince's word. Also, unlike hefting fish, I had no experience with jewelry. I didn't even know how many carats made an ounce.

I had bought only one diamond in my life and it was one-third carat and looked pretty big to me at the time. I still had that one. It was on an engagement ring that had been rejected.

From the sample lying glistening on my palm, I removed three stones, the largest, the smallest, and one that represented about the average of the sample. The smallest was bigger than the one-third carat reject I had at home. My plan was to have the three stones weighed and appraised to give me a handle on estimating the value of the whole stash.

It was a great relief to have the diamonds safe as we headed out of town. I had left my pickup in Vince's driveway. His Porsche had already been sold and the money deposited to the estate account, so we were using Vanessa's white Camry. I was driving since I was familiar with the Texas highways. The pines began to lose their majority to the hardwoods in the forested areas as we traveled farther south, and the rolling country began to flatten out.

On impulse, I put my hand into my trousers pocket and fetched out the three stones I had removed from the velvet bag while I was stashing it in the safety deposit box and handed them to Vanessa.

"Somehow I think these will be safer with you," I said.

She wrapped them in a tissue and stuffed it into her purse.

"Yes," she said, "I guess you are more likely to be mugged than me."

She turned on the radio, but after scanning the frequencies for awhile she couldn't find anything she liked so she turned it off. That suited me.

After a while she said, "I take it that *Gar* is short for *Garth,* or maybe *Garfield?*"

"I don't think so. If I remember correctly, Vince said that Paine's first name was something completely different, *Herman* I think. Some of his pals pinned that Gar nickname on Paine. They said the way he won money from his players reminded them of a garfish devouring mullets."

"Mullets or suckers?"

"They used to call poor players suckers, all right. For some reason they call them mullets, now. The meaning is the same, bait fish, small fish the big fish prey on. Anyway, Paine seemed to like it better than *Herman* so he started using it as his regular first name."

"So Gar Paine is one of the great poker players of the present generation?"

"No," I said, "I don't think even Benny makes that claim, although I'm sure Gar is good. He makes his money on running the game, games really. Actually, he's a casino operator. He takes a percentage of the pot on every round. His poker room is like a little chunk of Las Vegas. Gar doesn't actually play very much any more. Every table has a professional dealer who doesn't play, just deals. Well, the dealer also verifies that the bets are in and arbitrates any disputes between players. Gar doesn't play unless a table runs short on players and threatens to break up. Then he plays for awhile until more players come in."

"And running a casino is legal in Texas?"

"Not really. Texas law is a little vague on the issue. It's illegal to operate an 'open' game for profit. An open game is one that allows a stranger to join in after the game starts. Gambling for money is okay for people already acquainted so long as the operator doesn't make a profit."

"But Gar makes a profit."

"Yes. Everybody knows that but it's hard to prove. He gets to subtract his expenses from his gross receipts. And how would the district attorney know what his gross receipts are? If you ask the players how much they lost they will lie because they don't like to admit losing. Also, they don't want the game to be closed down. As far as expenses go, Gar has plenty, starting with the high rise apartment. He also furnishes liquor and other refreshments. When I was there he even had a good-looking hostess bringing the goodies around. So he can prove he has lots of expenses and they can't prove how much money he took in."

"So he's home free," Vanessa said.

"Yes and no. He has to put up with being raided by the police vice squad from time to time and spending a night or two in jail every once in a while. And he's in constant trouble with the Internal Revenue Service. They don't have to prove anything. When you deal with them the burden is on you to prove that you're innocent."

"So the IRS is after him for tax evasion?"

"I don't think so. If Gar is like other professional gamblers I know, he doesn't deny owing them what they claim. He just hasn't got around to paying it. They can't put him in the pen for that. At least that's the way I think the law works. Maybe the gamblers have to make small payments from time to time."

"So what does the IRS do to get their money from professional gamblers?"

"Well, they can garnishee wages and seize bank accounts. So these gentlemen—and I'm not saying all professional gamblers operate this way, probably some pay up—these gamblers don't have bank accounts or work for wages. They use cash entirely. They often have a roll of bills on them too big for a wallet."

It was well after the going home rush hour when we got to Houston, so driving through downtown wasn't much of a hassle. We had time for a leisurely dinner at one of the better restaurants before we got to Gar Paine's apartment. I felt that I was being scrutinized through the peephole after I knocked at the door. Finally the door opened a crack and, over a heavy-duty chain, somebody said, "What do you want?"

"Mike Kidd to see Gar Paine."

"Just a minute." And the door closed.

After about thirty seconds the door opened without the chain and a big man in an ill-fitting suit said, "Come on in."

He pointed toward the rear of the room and I saw Paine. He was gesturing for us to come over. The room was big. There were four full sized poker tables set up and three of them were being used. Benny, the small excitable man who had added zest to Vince's memorial service, was officiating at the farthest table from the door. He smiled and waved, and we both nodded at him. All the players were men except for two women, not sitting at the same table. One was young and overweight and the other looked to be in her sixties and was thin. There was a kitchen separated from the room by a bar set with snacks, including full-sized sandwiches. There were no bar stools. A good looking girl—not the same one I had seen last time—was taking bottled beers out of the refrigerator and setting them on a tray.

I shook hands with Paine and then introduced him to Vanessa. He looked her over in a manner not quite fitting his advanced age. I guess this was from habit as he had the reputation of being a woman chaser when he was younger. He seemed glad to see us, and invited us to sit down in one of the upholstered chairs surrounding a coffee table. The area seemed reserved for those who were taking a break from the games. He offered drinks and refreshments, but we had just had dinner and declined. After a few pleasantries, he got down to business.

"Vince gave me something to keep for you," he said.

Vanessa and I looked at each other, immensely relieved. "That's why we're here," I told him.

"He said that if you didn't come for it within three months after he died, I was to give it to some Dutch guy. I don't know what the hell it is, some kind of computer type thing. I don't do computers."

"And the Dutchman was named Van Moot?"

"Yeah, something like that. I've got it written down."

"Okay, you can give it to me now."

"Unfortunately," he said, "I don't have it here. It's at my home."

I could tell that I didn't have Gar Paine's entire attention. He was looking past me back toward the poker tables. I could tell that some type of altercation was taking place as the background noise had stopped and only a couple of voices could be heard, one of which was Benny's high-pitched tone and the other belonged to a player.

"Excuse me a minute," Gar Paine said.

We watched as he walked over to Benny's table.

"What's the trouble, Benny?"

Benny pointed to a pistol lying on the table next to a player's chips.

"This gentleman won't put that piece away," Benny said. "I told him a hundred times to keep it in his goddamn pocket, but he keeps hauling it out. I think he's just sore from losing and wants to make a fuss."

Gar Paine turned to the player, a middle-aged overweight man with a sweaty face. "What's the matter with you?" he said.

"There's nothing the matter with me. I have a license to carry this gun."

"That's called a concealed carry license. The key word is *concealed*. There are probably half a dozen men in this room right now carrying, but they have the good sense and good manners to keep their weapons concealed as required by law. Put your pistol away and don't let it be seen again."

"Suppose you make me." The fat player moved his right hand to within an inch of the weapon. The room went quiet and play stopped at all the tables.

"I tell you what," Gar said as he slowly brought his own auto-loader out of concealment. "I'll lay my weapon right here on the table and place my hand right here, about as close as your hand is to your weapon. Now, are you ready? Make your play, you son-of-a-bitch!"

The player stared at Gar for a several seconds. "Are you crazy?" he finally said.

"Yeah, that's what people say. Now I'm going to have Benny count to three and we'll both go for our guns."

"I'll put it away."

"You touch it and I'll assume you're drawing on me and I'll kill you."

"What do you want me to do?"

"What I want is for you to do is draw. But if you won't do that I want you to leave that weapon where it is and get your sorry ass out of here and never come back."

"What about my chips? What about my gun?"

"Back away from that weapon and Benny will cash you out. As for the gun, use it or lose it."

Slowly the man stood up and backed away from the table. Benny raked in his chips, sorted them and took cash out of a metal box and passed it to one of the players, who passed it on to the man. He crammed the bills into a pocket and turned and walked out of the apartment. Gar picked up the pistol and carried it over to the counter and laid it down among the snacks. The players went back to their games.

I had the weird feeling that I had just returned from a time trip to the late 1800s when Houston was part of the Old West. Either that or I had just stepped out of a John Wayne movie. Gar walked back to where Vanessa and I were standing.

"I have Vince's stuff over at my place," he said as if nothing unusual had just taken place. "I'll take you over there."

CHAPTER 22
GAR DELIVERS

We had no reason to return to the game, so instead of riding with Gar we followed him to his house on the northwest outskirts of Houston. He was driving a new Cadillac SUV that was easy to keep sight of. We found ourselves in a high middle-income neighborhood where Gar pulled into a driveway.

There was nothing distinctive about the house, but the yard stuck out as being both poorly kept and cluttered. Vanessa and I had to park on the street because a large bass boat with its trailer plus about a ten-year-old red Honda Civic took up the rest of the driveway. There was another boat, this one a pleasure speedboat on its trailer parked in the front yard.

Gar waited for us on the front porch and when we got there he unlocked the door with a key, opened it and called out, "Hey, Precious, I'm home!"

This call was immediately greeted by a deep and rumbling growl and the noise of canine claws slipping on hardwood floors as a huge pit bulldog charged to the opening and leaped into Gars arms and licked his face. Then the dog noticed Vanessa and me and sprang to the concrete floor of the porch, growling.

"No, no, Precious," Gar said. "Friends, friends."

The brute stopped his growling and moved closer, sniffing. I just then noticed that I had pulled Vanessa back and stepped between her and the dog without realizing what I was doing. I also discovered that I was grasping the butt of my handgun without realizing I had reached for it. It was still in the inside-the-waistband holster, but I was on the verge of drawing it. The movement to reach under the back hem of my jacket and grasp the handgun had been made automatic by practice. What surprised me was that I had also automatically moved to protect Vanessa. This must have been instinctive, something coded in the DNA.

"Don't worry," Gar said. "He's just a big overgrown puppy. He's so gentle he'll eat off your hand. All the way off up to the elbow" He laughed heartily at this display of humor although I had the feeling it was a stock line for him.

Gar pushed the door wide and stepped inside. The dog ran in and Gar turned and beckoned us to follow. He yelled out again, this time it was, "Betty!"

This brought a woman of late middle age from somewhere deeper in the house. She was blond and tall and must have been striking in her youth. Now she was in the process of losing her shape to middle age spread, and her face to wrinkles. The wrinkles might have been the result of heavy smoking, judging by the cigarette dangling from her lips and the heavy odor of tobacco in the house.

"What's the matter, now?" she said to Gar, "You're home early." Then, she spotted Vanessa and me and said, "Oh! Hello, I'm Betty Paine."

We took her hand by turn and introduced ourselves.

"They've come for that gadget that Vince Talbot left with me. Where is it?"

"That's Herman," she said. "He expects me to keep up with everything. Lord! He brings more junk home than a pawn shop, and I'm supposed to keep up with it."

I couldn't help but contrast the welcomes given Gar by Precious and Betty, and Gar responded in kind in both cases.

"That's why I put up with you," he said. "Find it. We don't want to keep these folks too long and I need to get back to the game."

The house was cluttered with various knickknacks and odds-and-ends. There were magazines stacked along both sides of the hallway, about fifty to the stack. At first I thought they were each a years worth of weeklies, but then I noticed that there was more than one kind to a stack. There were books everywhere.

"It looks like you're a big reader," I said.

"Hell, no; I'm just a big buyer of books."

"He thinks he can just absorb them," Betty said. "He can't get out of a book store without spending at least a hundred dollars. Then he stacks them up and hardly reads any of them."

154

"Why aren't you finding Vince's gadget?" Gar said. And Betty turned and walked out of the room, grumbling.

He led us into a big family room. It was as cluttered as the hallway and on every wall trophy heads of big game animals stared at us.

"Excuse the mess. Betty should have straightened things up better than this. I shot all these animals, but they represent only the best trophies. Do you hunt, Mike?

"Not big game, not anymore. I used to hunt deer but I always had a mixed feeling when I dropped one. There was elation mixed with remorse. With every kill the elation seemed to diminish and the remorse to grow, so I finally quit. I still hunt some, but birds only. Doves mostly, but also quail, and sometimes ducks."

"Yeah, I know what you mean. I don't hunt deer from a blind anymore, especially where they put out feeders. That just doesn't seem sporting like it once did. Nowadays I like to go to a wild area where no one has built any blinds. I like to search out the buck rubs and scrapes and find my own spot for an ambush. And like you say, the feeling of triumph gives way to a feeling of sadness. I let a dozen deer go by now for every one I kill. I just hunt for the trophy heads. That keeps that feeling of triumph higher than the regret."

"I do like bass fishing," I said. "It looks like you're into that."

"You mean those boats cluttering up the front. They're for sale. I took them from players who couldn't pay their losses. They represent bounced checks. I get a lot of stuff that way, and usually wind up selling it for a lot less than the credit I gave them. My own rig is at a marina up on Lake Fork right now. It's better than the one in the driveway. Lake Fork is up your way; maybe we could meet up there sometime."

"I'd be pleased to. Just give me a holler."

We went on this way, talking hunting and fishing and the equipment associated with these two subjects, guns and tackle. I broached subjects every once in awhile that I thought would interest Vanessa and bring her into the conversation. But Gar wouldn't bite. True to the profile of other women chasers I have known, Gar seemed to have little interest in women other than as sexual objects. After about thirty minutes Betty reappeared.

"For God's sake, Herman," she said. "You practically had this thing hidden where nobody could have found it. Is this the dingus you're looking for? It was in a little envelope with 'Vince' written on the outside."

She held out her hand, and sure enough there was a flash drive.

CHAPTER 23
I FOLD

It was after 2 a.m. when Vanessa and I pulled up into her driveway. As we had decided on the way back to Tyler, we stayed in the house only long enough for her to gather a few objects and a change of clothes. She would drive to Grandpa's house while I followed in the pickup. I was too tired to sit up all night again and neither of us wanted to spend another night in Vince's house until her new alarm system was installed.

Besides, since Buddy was already at Grandpa's I would have all my . . . what? All my loved ones? All my kith and kin? I wasn't sure what *kith* meant but maybe it included Vanessa. No, all my loved ones fitted best. Since Vince was gone Vanessa, Grandpa, and Buddy were the three people in the world that I cared most about. I would have all of them in one place to watch over.

There wasn't much traffic at that hour so it was easy for me to tag along in my truck behind her Camry and keep an eye on her. We pulled off Tyler's picturesque but bumpy red brick streets onto Highway 64 and headed east. I could feel the reassuring pressure of my 9 mm pistol against my back. I put my hand on my thigh and felt the flash drive through my trousers pocket to check that it was still there. On impulse, I put my hand into my pocket and pulled the drive out for brief inspection. I was eager to deliver it to Van Moot and get that worry off my back.

We were now out of town and moving at a good clip. My headlights picked up a whitetail deer, a doe. Apparently she had waited for Vanessa's car to pass and then darted across the highway right in front of my pickup. I was able to brake and swerve enough to miss her. When I straightened out the truck, it occurred to me that I had both hands on the wheel and no flash drive. That was worrisome but I told myself it was not a big deal. It had to be somewhere in the truck cab, if not on the floor boards then under one of the seats.

Suddenly there was a crash and a jar and the pickup was swerving. The rear view mirrors showed nothing but as I turned my head I saw on my left rear a large black pickup truck, bigger than mine, with its lights off. I was being pit maneuvered off the road.

The next thing I knew I was lying in a hospital bed listening to Grandpa telling Vanessa the story of my life.

CHAPTER 24
BENT BUT NOT BROKEN

The fog in my head was clearing. I could see Vanessa and Grandpa clearly. I could remember everything now up until I lost control of the truck. Evidently I had wrecked. The first thing I needed to know was how badly I was hurt. I tried moving my fingers. They responded, so I moved my hands. Vanessa was on her feet instantly and came to the bed.

"Take it easy, Mike."

I had a taste in mouth like rat droppings and it seemed to take me a little time to get my tongue working, but I finally got out, "How bad am I hurt?"

"Better not move until the nurse gets here. You were knocked out. You had a concussion. Lie still."

Vanessa must have pressed the call button because a middle-aged black nurse was soon hovering over me, checking my pulse, temperature, and whatever else was displayed on the wall monitor above my headboard. She told me not to move and left. A little later a doctor came in, another woman, a fairly young and rather attractive blonde. She looked over the vital signs and then shined a light in my eyes one at a time. By this time it seemed to me that I was thinking as clearly as I normally do.

"Do you know your name?" she said.

I started to say Napoleon Bonaparte to test her reaction, then thought better of it.

"Michael Kidd," I said.

She followed up with a string of other questions about where I live, what year it was, what month. I was doing fine until she asked the day of the week. When I said, "Saturday," she smiled at my answer, which was a day off.

"It's Sunday. You've lost a day. But not to worry. You've been unconscious for about twenty hours. I think you'll be fine but let's go real slow in getting you moving."

She lifted a bandage on my forehead to inspect whatever was underneath and then stuck it back down without comment. I was beginning to notice some aches here and there on my body and figured I'd have some bruises showing, if not now, soon.

She then had me move one limb at a time and finally to sit up. Eventually she had me walk a few steps while she pushed the IV stand along behind me. All the time Vanessa and Grandpa were watching me apprehensively but their expressions relaxed a little more with every move I made.

"I'm going to release you," the doctor said, "but you need to avoid any jolts or sudden moves for the next day or so. And call me or your regular doctor if you experience dizziness or nausea. I'll have a nurse remove the IV needle and the catheter. Then you can get dressed, but don't leave until they come for you with a wheel chair."

"I can walk okay."

"I know, but it's hospital procedure."

I guess that they make you leave in a wheelchair to keep you from hurting yourself on the way out and suing them. I was still feeling a little puny, so I didn't mind. Also, the hospital had been added onto continually over the years until it was something like a maze puzzle to find your way out. I had noticed the IV when I first woke up, but didn't realize I was hooked up with a bladder catheter until the doctor mentioned it. That's why she had me take only a few steps away from the bed.

It wasn't long before the same nurse came back into the room to take the needle out of my arm. I don't know why it took two of them to remove the catheter, but a second nurse, young brunette, came in to help with that job. I signaled Vanessa to leave the room for that minor ordeal and Grandpa went with her. Then the two nurses had me walk out into the hallway and up and down the corridor. They didn't touch me, but there was one on each side in case I started to fall. They had me walk back into the room and sit down on the bed to wait for the wheelchair. The black nurse handed me a prescription.

"The doctor says for you to get this filled only if the over-the-counter medicines like ibuprofen aren't effective for controlling the pain," she said as she handed me a computer-generated form.

When Grandpa, Vanessa, and I were alone in the room, Vanessa got my clothes out of the closet and turned her back while I got out of the skimpy wrap that hospitals use to humiliate you and into my own things again. Then the three of us just sat silently for a few minutes until my curiosity built up.

"Tell me what happened, Vanessa. The last thing I remember was a black truck running me off the road. It came up on me with its lights off."

"I got careless, I guess. I didn't notice you weren't behind me until I pulled up in Grandpa's yard. We waited about ten minutes for you and then we got back in my car and started looking for you. Your truck had plowed through some bushes and a fence. You could have been killed if you had hit a tree, but you tore down a fence one fencepost at a time, about six of them. Between the bushes and the posts and the fence wire, they stopped the truck without completely smashing it and you up.'

"Where's the truck?"

"I had them tow it out to my place," Grandpa said. "I didn't know whether you wanted it fixed or who you wanted to fix it. I don't think it's totaled, but it ain't going anywhere on its own for awhile."

"You did the right thing. Where's Buddy?"

"Buddy's out at my place. He'll be fine. I stocked up on books for him awhile back at the library annual sale. He's in hog heaven reading them."

Vanessa said, "Don't get excited, Mike, but when Grandpa and I got to the wreck you were lying on the ground with all your pockets turned out. They got the flash drive."

CHAPTER 25
JEAN'S CARAT PATCH

I didn't remember crashing the pickup, but I did remember having the flash drive in my hand shortly before I was forced off the road. I thought it must have fallen between the seats and then slid under one of them. The crooks probably looked in the glove compartment but I knew I hadn't put it there. Unless they had seen it lying on the floor boards, they didn't have it. With luck we would find it lodged somewhere under one of the seats.

I needed to talk to Van Moot. If he would just lay off the gangster tactics for awhile, I would get him the damned flash drive. But would it end there or would he assume that I had made a copy of the contents and come after me for that.

I was a little concerned that the thugs might want to search the wrecked pickup, assuming they hadn't already found the flash drive. It would probably take them some time to trace it to Grandpa's ranch, but just the thought of Buddy being alone was nagging at me, so, after warning him of the possibilities, I sent Grandpa ahead.

From the site of the crash Vanessa had gathered the objects from my pockets. She returned them to me along with the keys that had been dangling from the ignition lock. The thieves had found my 9 mm handgun and taken it. Thieves seem always to steal weapons when they get the chance. But they hadn't unhitched the inside-the-waistband holster from my belt, so Vanessa had that, too.

I hated to lose that pistol; it was sweet and I was very familiar with using it. But I had a replacement for it, the auto-loader I had taken from one of the thugs with the help of Grandpa and his walking stick. It was also a 9 mm and I would fire a few rounds through it at Grandpa's to make sure it was working all right. It was a genuine Berretta, so I knew it would fit the holster and be reliable.

When they wheeled me out of the front door at the hospital I had to sit there for a few minutes while Vanessa retrieved her car from the hospital parking lot. I felt better as soon as I was out of that wheelchair and sitting in the passenger's seat of the familiar white Camry.

"Where to?" Vanessa said, "Grandpa's?"

"No, my house. I want to be sure it hasn't been searched. Also I have another pistol there that will fit this holster fine. Then I want to go see a fellow I know, a jeweler. I want him to take a look at those gems I took from the stash. Do you have them on you?"

"Yes, they're still in my purse."

After I checked my house and re-armed myself, I directed Vanessa while she drove to the modest jewelry store owned by a fellow I was distantly related to. He was the husband of a second cousin of mine on my father's side.

"Jean's Jewelry," Vanessa said as she read the sign on the window, "Proprietor: Jean Hebert."

"Close enough," I said as I opened the barred door for her.

Jean was behind the counter fooling with a watchband. He looked up as we came in.

"Ah, Mike. Good to see you. But don't tell me you're here to rob me?"

"Hey, cousin. Why do you say that?"

"Well, you *are* packing heat, aren't you?"

"Yes, but how do you know?"

"Because you passed through my discreet metal detector and it flashed a little signal light here behind the counter. I just had it installed. I got tired of being robbed. When that little light comes on I fill my hand with this." He brought his hand up showing a large revolver. "I let them look around but I hold on to this baby all the time. This way I've got the drop on them."

"What if they ask you to open a case to show them something?"

"I tell them to come back when they're unarmed."

I couldn't blame him. He'd been robbed twice that I knew of, beaten up the first time and wounded the second. The man who wounded him had bled to death right about where I was standing, an artery cut by a bullet from the same .357 magnum revolver that was now lying on the counter top. Jean had been afraid that incident

166

would make his shop notorious and depress his business, but it had had the opposite effect. New customers as well as old had come in to congratulate him for performing a public service.

"Vanessa," I said, "this is my cousin-in-law, Jean Hebert." I pronounced his name the French way, "zhawn a bear." I knew he preferred that although most of his customers pronounced it "jeen heeburt." In fact, one branch of his family had taken on the English pronunciation even among themselves. Jean was authentic Cajun from Southern Louisiana and had a trace of the accent. He could speak French, at least the Cajun dialect French which, I suppose, sounds archaic to a modern Frenchman.

"Glad to meet you, Vanessa," Jean said. Then he did a double take on my face.

"Jesus, Mike, it looks like you finally met your match in a fist fight."

"Minor car accident," I said. "Let me have the rocks, Vanessa."

When she handed me the little bundle of tissue paper I unwrapped it and set the three diamonds on the counter.

"Well, well," he said.

He was already wearing a jeweler's loupe. He pulled it down in front of his eye and carefully inspected the stones, one at a time. Finally he shoved the loupe back up on his forehead toward his short curly blond hair and looked up at me.

"And? What do you want me to do with them?"

"First of all, I want to know if they're genuine diamonds."

"No doubt about that."

"Could they be synthetic?"

"Natural. They are almost sure to have been mined, but we can find out pretty quickly."

Again the loupe came down and the inspection was resumed. Then Jean took a small lamp out of a drawer, plugged it in, and held it next to each stone for another examination.

"They're not synthetic. The UV light confirms it, but I already knew for two reasons. First, cultured diamonds of gem size are engraved by the manufacturer. But beside that the largest gem, this fat rascal, is cut in a way that went out of fashion in the 1930s when the cutters found another facet arrangement gives more brilliance than this one. No one cuts a diamond like this anymore. It was cut long before the existence of synthetic diamonds. I'd guess these are inherited and have been in somebody's family for a long time."

Vince, you clever dickens. You used a facet design that would shout mined.

"As a matter of fact, they *are* inherited. Next question, what are they worth?"

"To me or to you?"

"I guess to you. I don't want to sell them right away, but if I did what could I expect to get for them?"

Jean pulled out a small balance and weighed them individually.

"What you have here is a one carat, a ten carat, and a twenty carat. Despite what you may hear about diamonds being a good investment against inflation, the catch is, unless you are a jeweler, you have to buy them at retail and sell them at wholesale."

"How much is a carat?"

"A carat is two-tenths of a gram. That's *carat* with a *c. Karat* spelled with a *k* is completely different. It applies to gold and one *k*-karat is one twenty-fourth gold. Pure gold is 24 karat."

"Well, back to diamonds, give me a rough figure for the value—what I could expect to get— for diamonds. How much per carat?"

Jean pursed his lips. "See, it doesn't work that way. A two carat diamond is worth more than twice as much as a one carat diamond and so on. That's because they are increasingly rare according to size. Let's see with these stones. If you wanted to sell them to me, I'd probably give you $400 for the one carat, $8,000 for the ten carat, and $40,000 for the twenty carat. I would give you even more for the big one but for the fact that I would have to spend a couple thou having it re-cut to a modern pattern to bring it to its maximum value. If you're really interested in selling the big one, you'll need to give me time to arrange a loan from my bank."

He looked at me quizzically, evidently expecting me to say something. But I was doing some mental calculations. I know how to do integral calculus and even can solve simple differential equations, but was never good at regular arithmetic, especially mental arithmetic.

I knew that a kilogram was approximately two pounds, so I had about 1 kilogram of diamonds. Taking the price of $1,000 per carat as the average value would not be far off and it would make calculations simpler. So my one kilogram of diamonds was 1,000 grams. Dividing that by 0.2 grams per carat was the same as multiplying by 10 and dividing by 2. That made 5,000 carats total in the velvet bag. Five thousand carats at $1,000 per carat was $5,000,000. What I had in my safety deposit box was five million dollars worth of diamonds!

Then, noticing Jean was waiting for an answer I said, "If I decide to sell I'll give you plenty of time to arrange a loan."

"Have you already sold any of your inherited stones?" Jean asked. "The big one wasn't one of a pair by any chance?"

"No, this is all there was." I hated to lie but I certainly wasn't going to advertise that I had a stash of diamonds. Besides, it wasn't one of a pair; it was one of a couple of dozen.

"I just wondered. A Dallas jeweler I know bought an old-cut twenty-carat a few weeks ago. I didn't see it but the way he described it sounded like a twin to yours."

CHAPTER 26
FRESH DECK

The first thing Vanessa and I saw as we pulled up in Grandpa's front yard was my sad looking pickup. The front end was pretty well smashed. The hood was bent up in the middle and I was itching to take a look at the engine, but that would have to wait. The air bag had gone off all right and it was probably why I was walking today and not still laid up in the hospital. The door was still working, and the thugs had evidently released my seat belt and dragged me out of the cab to search me. As I was making my inspection Grandpa and Buddy came out and stood watching me.

It didn't take long to spot the flash drive wedged under the springs of the passenger seat. It took a little longer to get it out though because my hand and forearm were too big to reach very far through the narrow opening under the seat. I was about ready to get some wrenches and remove the seat when Vanessa reached in and was able to get it out.

"It looks in good shape," she said.

"What is it?" Grandpa said.

"It's a flash drive. It stores computer data. You plug it into a computer to read or write to it. Vince wanted that Van Moot guy to have it. I figure that once we deliver it to him we'll be out of danger."

We all seemed to want to drop the subject until after dinner. Then, still sitting around the table after we had carried the dishes to the sink, we began to fill one another in on our thoughts about the matter. By this time I thought I had a pretty good idea of what I had destroyed when I burned that briefcase down by the creek, and I laid my cards out for inspection.

"Finding the diamonds has made this situation a new game with a fresh deck. Now we know what Van Loon has been after. He wants the plans for Vince's diamond-growing rig, and he wants assurance that there aren't any other copies of those plans floating around. Grandpa and I must have burned all the paper plans of the diamond growing device—the final plans plus a bunch of working papers and some CDs, everything relating to the device. The flash drive must be the equivalent of the briefcase we destroyed. Now our problem is that even after I give the flash drive to Van Moot, he might think that I had made a copy of it."

"Hell," Grandpa said, "For all he knows you still have the briefcase somewhere. And can't you plug that gizmo into your own computer and make a dozen copies? For all he knows, you already have."

"That's the problem. He can't ever be sure."

"Well, if you've got the name you might just as well have the game."

"How's that, Tom?" Vanessa said.

"I mean you might as well hang for wolf as a sheep. Hell, you young people don't even know the sayings of your own culture. I'll spell it out. Since this Van Derhoot fellow thinks you have made copies, you might as well make one. Hell, make a dozen. Tell Van Shoot that they'll spout up all over if he doesn't lay off. Otherwise, when he gets this one original gizmo he's liable to have you killed."

"If he wanted me dead they could have easily killed me when they laid me out unconscious on the ground."

"That's what I mean. They want you alive up to time they get the gizmo. After that they might just as soon you were dead."

I had been thinking along the same lines as Grandpa, and if he had a computer in his house I would have made a copy of whatever was on the flash drive right then. But there was still a missing piece to the puzzle.

"Van Moot told me that he had reason to believe that the contract had been broken. Why would he say that? I hadn't tried to sell any of the diamonds; I didn't even have them then. He started the rough stuff before Buddy had put the jigsaw puzzle together."

"That was a hard one," Buddy said. "Captain Kidd's buried treasure."

"The only thing Van Moot could have had against me at the time those toughs came at us on the sidewalk was that I had not yet provided him with the stuff in the briefcase and on this flash drive. But he acted as if something had happened, not that something had failed to happen. What could that have been?"

Grandpa slapped his hand on the table. "Somebody sold some diamonds! Diamonds with an old-fashioned cut that nobody has used since the 1930s."

That made sense. We looked at one another and nodded. Even Buddy nodded. Vanessa summed it up. "The new game is to find out who got hold of Vince's device, or the plans to his device, and went into business for himself. To get Mike in the clear we've got to find the thief and hand him over to Van Moot."

CHAPTER 27
HARD TO FIND

It was early afternoon of the next day when I got back to DataDigm. Antoinette tried not to show her curiosity about my bruised face as I walked into the foyer. She was decked out as usual in a long-sleeved dark blouse that made her slim frame look even thinner, almost skinny and yet still attractive.

"Minor car accident," I said without stopping to give any specifics.

I had driven into the parking lot with a new, dark maroon Avalon sedan rented from the Toyota dealer. My truck was at the same dealer getting reconstructed. It would take about a week, they said. Insurance would pay for the repairs. The rental was on me.

Ensconced once again in my office, I called Jack McKinney. He said give him about ten minutes and he would be there. I spent those ten minutes reviewing my endeavor to get Grandpa to agree to move into town. I wanted Grandpa, Buddy, and me all to move into Vince's house along with Vanessa. That way I would have all my eggs in one basket and we could all keep an eye out for one another. Vanessa was all for it, mostly, I supposed, because she was afraid to stay in Vince's old house alone. I knew Buddy would rather stay at my house or Grandpa's because he didn't like things to change, but I was sure I could persuade him. Grandpa had reacted just about as I had expected.

"Well, I sure don't mean to hurt anybody's feelings, but I just can't let anybody scare me off my own property. I wouldn't be able to look myself in the mirror. I'll just stay here and hope and pray they show up so I can teach them some manners. Besides, I've got my horses to take care of."

"Grandpa," I said, "I'll talk to your neighbor. You've had his son do some chores before. I'll pay him to feed the horses and whatever else needs doing."

I hated to do it, but when he started shaking his head again I played the trump card. "You did promise to back me up when I need you. I need you, Grandpa. I can't be with Vanessa and Buddy all the time."

That got him, of course. So we had spent the morning moving Buddy and Grandpa into Vanessa's house. The back door had been repaired and a good alarm system installed. There were four bedrooms, one for each of us, and the one closest to Vanessa's was designated my room for purposes of decorum although I think Grandpa was fully aware that I would be sleeping with Vanessa.

Buddy didn't like it at first but when he discovered Vince's library he settled down. Vince's extensive book collection included lots of technical works that were right up Buddy's alley, although I could never figure out why. His reaction to Vince's puzzles surprised me. Some he figured out instantly, while even the object of others seemed completely beyond his understanding.

Jack McKinney stopped my musing by entering the room.

"My God! What happened to you?"

"Minor car accident. I'm okay; it looks worse than it feels. Jack, do you remember an early contract with the army that required building a diamond substrate?"

"Hmmm, let me think. Yeah, Vince did most of the work himself but I helped some along with others. That was one of our first substantial contracts. What about it?"

"What happened to the equipment that was used to grow the substrate?"

"If I remember correctly we offered all the equipment to the army since they paid for it. They declined, which is usual, and we scrapped it, which is usual."

This came as a disappointment, but I kept digging. "By scrapping, what do you mean? You dumped it?"

"No, we don't waste anything that might be used to build something else out of. Old stuff like that goes in the junkyard. When our machinists or electronic technicians need some gears or switches or something, we encourage them to take a look in the junkyard to see if there is something they can use before they order something new. Saves both time and money. We salvaged a power supply not long ago from the junkyard."

"Well, where is the junkyard?"

"Follow me."

And he led me back through the military contracts section, through the machine shop with its drill presses and milling machines, into a supply room where sheet metal of various kinds was stacked along with wooden two-by-fours and plywood. Cans of solvents and paints and glues were neatly stacked along with an assortment of other chemicals. There was a lifting door to the outside where supplies could be brought in from delivery trucks.

At first I thought that Jack would stop here, but he opened a door that led into a large area that was not nearly as neat. Here were wheels, axles, odds and ends of every type, most dirty. It too had an overhead door to the outside.

"This is what we call the junkyard, although, as you can see, it really is a junk room."

"Do you have any idea where that diamond growing equipment would be?"

"If it's still here I guess it would be in the electronics section," he said, walking between rows of mechanical parts. The only order seemed to be that electronic stuff was in its own area, and we paused there while Jack surveyed the jumble of electronic parts, black boxes, glass containers and other stuff.

I thought I had been everywhere in the building except for a couple of rooms where work was done for which I had no need-to-know and even my SECRET clearance wouldn't admit me, but I had never been in the junkyard before.

"I don't see any sign of that carbon evaporation equipment," McKinney said. "Some stuff is simply thrown out if it doesn't seem to have any possible future use, but I don't think that diamond substrate thing would fall into that category. Not all of it, anyway."

"What's in there?" I pointed to a door in the back with a security keyboard lock.

"That's a holding room. A lot of the stuff in the junkyard was first put in there in case we got an extension or a follow-on contract. Or because we were trying to get a new contract that the equipment could be used for."

"Let's have a look."

Jack walked up to the door and stared at the combination lock. He keyed in a combination but the lock didn't respond. He tried again. And then again. "It doesn't come back to me. It's been too long since I worked this lock. I must have forgotten the combination."

"Would this be one of those rooms that I couldn't enter because of a need-to-know?"

"I wouldn't think so. You should be able to get the combo from Carl. I could get it and we could look together if you want to."

"Do you think that carbon evaporation stuff is in there?"

"It could be, or it could have been cannibalized long ago. I think that Vince had a laser connected to it somehow, maybe to spot evaporate the carbon or polish the diamond film produced by the evaporation process. I don't think that would have been trashed."

"I'd appreciate it if you would do that, get the combination and give me a tour."

"Sure thing. I'll see Carl and get back to you. That's a much smaller room though, so it won't be much of a tour." After a pause he added, "What makes you interested in that old equipment?"

It was a natural question, but I sensed something a little unnatural in Jack McKinney's voice.

"Something I found in Vince's notes," I said. "It made me think he had plans for it."

CHAPTER 28
MARTIN KNOWS

Almost as soon as I returned to my office Jack McKinney called to tell me that Carl Hindman had left early that afternoon and so Jack was not able to let me into the newly discovered room.

"Tomorrow will be all right," I said, trying to sound indifferent. Actually, I was sorely disappointed. The truth was that I was eaten up with curiosity about that room.

The only thing that made sense to me was that someone had recently sold some diamonds made by Vince's contraption or one like it. That's why Van Moot claimed the contract—the oral contract, not anything in writing—had been broken. That unwritten contract was that Vince would not sell any more diamonds or reveal the knowledge of how he had made the diamonds to anyone. Now Van Moot was holding me to that same contract, and the appearance on the market of some, or at least one, of these diamonds meant to Van Moot that I had broken that contract.

If someone knew about Vince's diamond factory, it made sense to me that it would be someone at DataDigm. And if that person had decided to go into business for himself he would have to be a fast worker to construct a brand new device and get it working just a few days after Vince's death. No, the original machine must still be intact, and I was betting that it was stored somewhere on the premises. Where better than in a seldom used locked room such as the one entered only from the junkyard?

I took the flash drive out of my pocket and inspected it. I was wondering if delivering it to Van Moot would now be sufficient or would he want me to pay in blood for what he thought was my breach of contract. I had told Vanessa and Grandpa that I would make copies of it and tell Van Moot that they would crop up like toadstools after a rainy week if anything happened to me.

I swung my chair to face the desktop computer. I turned it on and pulled a new CD from its box. I inserted the CD in the drive and located the USB port into which I could connect the flash drive. I hesitated. A thought had suddenly occurred to me.

I laid the flash drive on the desk and dialed Jack McKinney again. He immediately picked up.

"Jack, who is the number one computer wizard at DataDigm?"

"Martin Spencer," he said without hesitation. "He codes in all known computer languages and is our interface expert, interface between soft- and hardware."

"I can't place him, but I must have seen him. Would you please locate him and send him to my office?

"Sure thing."

It was getting close to quitting time when I heard a soft knock on the door. Before I could call out to come in, the door opened and Martin Spencer walked in. I immediately remembered having seen him, even shaken his hand on one of my rounds of the facility. I stood up and signaled him to come up to the desk and sit down.

We sat sort of appraising each other for a few seconds. I smiled. He smiled back.

"Martin, I understand that you are our number one computer guru."

He smiled again and nodded. His face reminded me of portraits of Christ, the benign smile, auburn hair and beard, and blue eyes that seemed to say that he had seen everything and understood everything.

But a glance at the rest of him dispelled the mystic aura of his face. He was of medium height but must have weighed 300 pounds. His shoulders sloped and his hips were disproportionately large, barely fitting between the arms of his chair. His hands, in his lap with short tapered fingers interlaced, were large and pale with the nails either clipped or bitten very short. He wore a long-sleeved, striped dress shirt but no tie. The shirt had pockets on each side and each pocket had a plastic protector that bulged with pencils, pens, rulers, calculators, notepads, screw drivers, and various small tools that I wasn't familiar with.

I held up the flash drive.

"My question is, can I load a device like this with data and make it so that it would show if anyone had ever uploaded it to a computer?"

"I doubt it."

"You mean there's no way a flash drive can be coded so that a person could tell if it had been read from before?"

"That's a different question," Spencer said. "You first asked if you could arrange a flash drive to do that. I said I doubt it because if you could you wouldn't need to ask me. Your second question is probably what you meant in the first place. Can such a thing be done? The answer to that is yes. A device like that flash drive could be coded so that if you plugged it into a computer and opened it, the first thing you would see on the monitor screen would be a statement such as, 'This device has previously been opened blank times,' with the blank filled in by the appropriate number."

I was put off by his manner but intrigued by his answer. I found myself thinking about Buddy and my previous observation that autism and genius were related.

"Are you sure?" I don't know why I asked; he was sure of everything he said.

"Yes, I coded a flash drive for Vince to do exactly that. It looked just like the one you're holding."

CHAPTER 29
HOLE CARD

The rest of that day I spent in my office mulling over the situation. I now found myself on the horns of a dilemma, or in plain talk, between a rock and a hard place. I couldn't make a copy of what was on the flash drive, but if I didn't I wouldn't have any insurance against being knocked off by one of Van Moot's crew once I handed over the drive.

I thought about Martin Spencer. He could probably figure out how to save the data from the flash drive and then fix it so that it still indicated that it had never been opened. The more I thought about it the surer I was that DataDigm's guru and certified genius could pull that off. He could off-load the data, rework his coding on this or a new flash drive, and load it back.

However, I was fairly sure that someone in the company had already pirated Vince's invention and might be eager to have the contents of the flash drive. Whoever was involved had the equipment but I had the operating manual on the flash drive. Martin seemed honest but so did everyone else in the place. Vince had trusted Martin, but he had also trusted all the other employees, and one of them must have betrayed that trust. I decided not to trust any of them.

One thing about being the boss, I could come and go on my own schedule. Carl Hindman had provided me with a key to the front door so that I could get in and out after hours. There was a double lock and the night watchman had to work the other from the inside to let you in, but you could leave without his help. Carl said that Vince often worked until everyone else had left and the night watchman had come on duty. I was not a workaholic like Vince, but I thought I might like to do some more searching after hours sometime. Right now it was quitting time, and I stayed at my desk until most of the employees had left.

I sat, trying to think of a new angle, couldn't come up with anything and left the building. Martin Spencer was just getting into his little car when I got to the parking lot. It was about a twenty-year old faded brown Mazda with a cracked side window. I walked over to him.

"Martin, did Vince give you any other unusual assignments beside the flash drive?"

"He might have, but that's the only thing that comes to mind. I helped him out a couple of times with computer problems at his house. That was on my own time as a favor. Gurus do a lot of gratis work for friends. I'm afraid it goes with the territory."

"But no big jobs?"

"No, just things like helping him with his DSL connection, and later with his wireless router. At work, I do trouble shooting of that type for all the equipment. Most of it is so simple that I have to wonder if the people with the problems are lazy rather than stupid."

"I wouldn't call Vince either stupid or lazy."

"Oh, I don't mean Vince. He was highly intelligent. There are a handful of really intelligent people at DataDigm, and Vince was one of them. With him it was a matter of efficiency. He knew a lot about computers and computing, but he was always busy and his time was simply worth more than my time, monetarily speaking."

I somehow got the impression that he did not include me in that handful of sharp pencils. I also got the impression that if he were to name those deep thinkers his own name would top the list. In spite of his oblique insults I was beginning to like the man. His frankness was refreshing. I was also beginning to think that he might have been involved with Vince in programming the diamond machine. After all, Vince had said in the note he left with the diamonds that he had help with the device. Martin just might be my ace-in-hole in the game I'd been forced to be playing.

"You go out for lunch?" I said.

"Yes."

"Want to have lunch with me tomorrow?"

"That would be nice."

"Come by my office around noon."

CHAPTER 30
LUNCH POETRY

I had a little shopping to do before I got to the office the next day, so it was mid morning when I got Jack McKinney on the phone.

"Okay, Jack," I said, "I'm ready to see that back storage room if you're ready to show it to me."

"I told Carl about needing the combination and he said he'd come by and bring it to me, but so far he hasn't."

"Okay, I'll give Carl a call."

But Carl didn't answer so my next call was to Antoinette. "Carl came in at eight," she said, "But he left again just a few minutes ago, shortly after you got here. I'm sure he'll be back. Do you want me to tell him you're looking for him when he gets back?"

"No, Antoinette. Just let me know when he gets back." I wasn't sure why, but I added, "No need to say anything to him about it."

I sat at the desk wondering about the instructions I had just given Antoinette. I reached out and pulled one of the executive toys that lay within reach. It was a row of ten pendulums set close together with the bobs touching. The bobs were steel ball spheres, produced to be ball bearings. I pulled one of the end bobs out and released it. It smacked into the next steel ball but that one didn't move; none of them did except the last one on the end. It flew out and when it fell back the impact was passed through the line of balls back to the one I had first lifted. And so the apparatus oscillated, with only the balls on each end appearing to move at all.

Conservation of momentum, I thought. The momentum of the first ball is transferred to the next and so on to the last, which was free to move. Conservation of energy, too, was shown by the fact that the end balls rose each time almost to the level of the previous flight. I stopped the motion and started over, this time lifting two balls together. Predictably, there was no movement except for the two steel balls that swung out at the other end.

Vince had a Ph.D. in physics, and this was the kind of toy a physicist would enjoy. I wished I had taken more physics courses at the university. I had taken a couple at the junior college, but not much besides math at the university. I knew practically nothing about lasers, and wondered if I would recognize one if I found it in the holding room.

I didn't like being frustrated about getting into that room. I couldn't help but wonder if Jack McKinney really did remember the combination, but didn't want me nosing around in there. There didn't seem to be any reason to keep the door locked, anyway, if it really held only stuff waiting to be scrapped. Okay, maybe they needed to lock up the stuff that could be cannibalized to build new stuff until they were sure it was only scrap. But it looked to me as if they could keep it safe from the machinists by simply tagging it. I knew that the odds were that I wouldn't find any of Vince's carbon vaporizing equipment in there but I also felt that the longer I delayed in getting into that room the lower those odds would become.

I was still fiddling with the pendulum gadget when a soft knock sounded on my door, immediately followed by the entrance of the corporate guru, Martin Spencer. He took a few steps and stopped, standing there smiling at me with his saintly face. I almost felt that I was receiving a blessing. I needed one.

"Lunch time," he said.

He was dressed exactly as yesterday, including the bulging shirt pockets and khaki trousers. No, not exactly the same. I think yesterday's shirt had thin blue stripes while this one had thin red ones. There was nothing slovenly about his clothes or his person, but I had a mental picture of a clothes closet filled with khaki trousers and long sleeved, double pocketed, white pinstriped shirts. I imagined him thoughtfully choosing between thin blue stripes to match his eyes or dark red stripes to match his hair. His shoes were brown leather. His socks were white.

I had not forgotten our lunch date; in fact, I had told Vanessa that I wouldn't be able to see her for lunch. The time had slipped by me, however, and I glanced up at Vince's Monopoly clock. Sure enough, the little capitalist was pointing straight up with both arms. So I got up and Martin and I walked out of the building together. Since I had invited him I thought I should drive, so we headed for the dark maroon Avalon. I told him where we were going and asked if that was all right.

He nodded and said, "Fine."

It was a sandwich shop with booths. I chose it more for its suitability to having a conversation than for the quality of the food, not that there was anything wrong with the food. I had noticed a few days ago when Vanessa and I had met for lunch that we could actually hear each other without shouting, a rare thing in a restaurant nowadays. The secret seemed to lie in the fact that the kitchen was completely separated from the dining space. You couldn't even catch a glance of the kitchen or hear the usual clatter of china. You gave your order, paid, and took a number to your table and after a while a waitress brought your order.

I had to remind myself to pay for both orders. I was still not used to being affluent. Also, I was the boss and had invited one of my employees to lunch. I had to break the going Dutch habit.

"Have you eaten here before?" I asked.

"Yes, I always eat out and have tried almost all the restaurants, at least all that are fast enough to allow me to get back to work at a reasonable time. The recipes here are simple but the ingredients are of good quality."

"I personally prefer simple food. In the words of the poet, 'a loaf of bread a jug of wine . . . and thou beside me' is enough. But I think he should have included a slab of cheese."

"I had always presumed he was talking to a slab of cheese."

This was my introduction to Martin's odd sense of humor and to the fact that he was a bona fide gourmet. He was also a gourmand, as he not only knew about fine foods but was a hearty eater of them. Apparently, his favorite topic of conversation was food, and when our sandwiches arrived he treated me to a discussion of the origins of different sandwich recipes, and in which restaurants in which cities they had originated. He gave me the histories and distinguishing characteristics of *hoagies, heroes, grinders, submarines,* and *po' boys.*

Since he was doing most of the talking I finished eating first. "Martin, did you work with Vince on the carbon evaporation chamber contract?"

"No. That contract came in before I started at DataDigm."

Damn! I had hoped he could provide something useful.

Martin took a bite, chewed it slowly, and washed it down with iced tea. "However, I did some programming work for Vince in regard to the laser beam within the chamber."

"That's what I meant."

"Oh, I thought you asked if I had worked on the contract. My work wasn't charged to the contract."

"What did you charge to?"

"Concept Development. A lot of corporate profit is set aside to work on ideas that might result in contract proposals or somehow bring in money."

"Did Vince tell you how your program would be used?"

"No, he seemed to avoid telling me very much."

"Do you think that it was to be used to direct a laser?"

"No."

Again I was disappointed. But I remembered Martin's habit of being literal, so I rephrased the question. "Did you think it had any connection to a laser?"

"Yes, he wanted a program that would produce certain output that would turn a laser on and off while simultaneously orienting a small stage or platform in front of the laser beam. He said something about shaping and polishing lenses, something about scratch-proof lenses for space applications."

I thought that over while Martin finished off the last of his sandwich and carefully cleaned his face with a paper napkin. "But I don't think that was what he really wanted to do."

"And what was that?"

"It looked to me as if he planned on growing gem quality diamonds and shaping their facets with the laser beam."

He smiled. But this time he didn't look to me like a saint. He looked like the cat that ate the canary.

CHAPTER 31
CARDS FACE-UP

We were through eating but by no means through talking. I checked my watch and Martin seemed to take that as a hint that it was time to get back to the office and started to get up, an action impeded by the close fit of his body between the bench and the table.

"No hurry," I said. "I want to hear more about this program of yours."

Martin settled back into position. "To which contract should I charge my time after the hour allotted for lunch?"

"Concept Development. But I haven't noticed employees being sticklers about lunch hours, or starting and stopping hours, either. Not that I want to change those habits which must have been approved by Vince."

He chuckled. "Fair enough. And speaking of that, two employees just came in, saw us, turned around and left without ordering anything."

"Rally? Who?"

"Carl Hindman and Antoinette Black. I don't think they are aware that I noticed them. But regarding your question about my program for Vince, what do you want to know?"

I paused to digest what Martin had just told me. Was there something romantic between

Antoinette and Carl? No one was held to a strict time to lunch. Antoinette had only to make sure that someone was at her station and there was no reason I could think of that would embarrass them for me to see them together. I remembered that Carl had said his wife had moved out, and I wondered if Antoinette could figure in that. I knew that some companies frowned on romance between employees. I'd have to check on whether DataDigm had such a policy. But right now I wanted to ask Martin something.

"What makes you think that Vince wanted to try making gem-quality diamonds?"

"Well, he kept after me to include lots more comments in the coding than I was used to—"

"You can include comments within the code?"

He looked at me as if I had just fallen off a turnip truck. "You really don't know anything about programming at all?"

I refused to be insulted. "That's your clue to use simple language."

"I can see that. Well, each line of code is like a sentence instructing the computer on what to do. But you can place any number of lines within the program that the computer will skip over. This is providing you start the line with a character designated to tell the computer to ignore this line and skip to the next. Because the chief use of these ignored lines is to make comments, they are called comment lines or just comments."

"And their purpose is . . . ?" This earned me another look of disgust.

"There are two reasons for comments. Well, three if you count blank lines inserted just to make the program easier to read. The first main reason is to remind the programmer what he is about to instruct the computer to do or perhaps has just done. The longer and more complicated the program, the more the programmer uses comments to help him in constructing the program. The second reason is to help some other person to understand the program in case changes should later be needed to adapt the program to new or expanded uses. Often programs grow by additional code supplied by different programmers to handle a similar but more complex problem."

"So there was nothing unusual about Vince asking you to use lots of comments?"

"Yes, there was. Because of my superior programming abilities, I need very few comments to remind myself of what the code is doing. Vince knew that. But he never asked me before or later to add comments to a program. Obviously, he intended to make changes after I finished my job."

"Then Vince was capable of programming?"

"Sure. Most engineers and scientists can do some programming. Vince could have written the program himself, although it would not have been an elegant job. It would have been crude but effective. I'm sure he used me to write the foundation of the program just as a matter of efficiency. I could have it finished by the time he was barely getting started."

It was now after one o'clock and the lunch crowd was beginning to thin out. I was excited but tried to show only casual interest. "Was there a particular part of the program where Vince wanted you to put in a lot of comments?"

"Yes."

"And what part was that?"

"The part that defined the top, or face. He had me program a simple four-sided pyramid, but he obviously planned to make a much more complicated structure of intersecting planes and needed to know how to define each intersection. He also had me program a smooth spherical shape, but I think that was to make me believe he was interested in lenses rather than gem facets."

"Did Vince actually use your program?" I remembered Martin's tendency to be literal so I added, "I mean, did he ever to your knowledge try to produce gemstones?" I didn't want to hear about using the program as a door stopper.

"I can't say for sure. I believe he attempted it, but that's only a guess."

"Was it generally believed at DataDigm that Vince was experimenting with producing gemstones?"

"Of course I can't say what others believed, but I don't recall hearing anyone say anything along those lines. Vince was always fooling around with different devices. In this case we had a piece of equipment that did the job it was built to do, and he wanted to see if it could be extended to some other purpose. There was nothing unusual about that except for the romance associated with diamonds."

"Where did he do this fooling around with discarded equipment?" I asked.

"Wherever they were located if that space wasn't needed for an active contract. If the space was needed he would sometimes have it moved into the storage room next to the junkyard. Then he would tinker with it and sometimes come up with an idea for a new contract or a follow up."

I felt a thrill of anticipation. "Is that what he did with the carbon evaporation equipment?"

"Yes, he did. And he was in there a lot at the time he came to me for programming help. We already knew how to grow a diamond film with that equipment and he wanted something that looked like it could facet a gemstone, so I put two and two together."

After that neither Martin nor I said anything for awhile. We just looked at each other. Martin's face was inscrutable but visions of diamonds danced in my head. I was thinking that I needed to tell the whole story to someone. I wondered if Vince had gone to Martin for help because he was the champion programmer or because he had trusted him more than anyone else. And if Vince had trusted him did that mean I could, too?

But someone at DataDigm had betrayed Vince. At least that's the way it looked to me. Someone had revived the instrument and had gone into the jewelry business with it. But that someone probably didn't know how to change the facet design from the last one that Vince had used. And that was the old-fashioned one that was an advantage to Vince at the time but was now a giveaway.

Martin was evidently not the type who felt embarrassed by long silences in a conversation. Apparently he would sit there silent until I said something or he remembered some esoteric fact about cooking he wanted to share with me.

If my theory was right, he was not the underground gem maker because he would know how to change the program to set up another facet design. He wouldn't stick with the antique pattern that was easy to spot. Also, I had observed that Martin was one of those who often stayed after hours. He might be able to tell me who had been going into the storage room at night since Vince had entered the hospital for the last time. Martin's eyes glittered and I thought I read something in that pleasant face.

"Martin," I said, "is there something else you want to tell me?"

"As a matter of fact, I was wondering if you would like to know the story behind the famous Philly cheese-steak sandwich."

CHAPTER 32
SCHOOL DAYS

My lunch with Martin Spencer had its highs and lows. No doubt he was a genius but his mental powers seemed focused on computer programming and culinary art. I felt I had learned all I was going to get from him that would be helpful. There were questions that I needed to ask but not of Martin or anyone else at DataDigm. I felt sure that someone there had used Vince's contraption to make some diamond gemstones, and too many questions on my part would put that person on guard.

I cursed my ignorance and thought of the courses I could have taken at Tyler Junior College or the University of Texas at Tyler. Of course, if I had known I was going to inherit a high tech business I would have gotten a degree or at least an education in science or engineering. Or business management.

Thinking about some of the courses I had taken in my erratic scholastic career, one of my teachers came to mind. After dropping Martin off at DataDigm I drove over to pick up Buddy, then to the campus of Tyler Junior College.

TJC was more like a university than its name suggested. From its humble beginning it had grown both physically and educationally so that it now offered a large menu of freshman and sophomore courses and two-year associate degrees. Over the years I had taken enough courses from a particular physics professor that I had come to know him fairly well. He taught physics courses at the university as well, but he was usually to be found at the junior college. It was almost two o'clock when Buddy and I stood before a door marked, "Professor Buford Goodson." I knocked.

"Come in," he said.

He hadn't changed since I saw him last, a small man with a slight build, a patrician face and curly white hair. He was seated behind a light complexioned oak desk wearing a suit complete with buttoned-down collar and tie. He looked up and I could tell he remembered me, but he'd never seen Buddy before.

"I'm Michael Kidd. I've taken courses from you, but not in the last couple of years. This is my younger brother, Buddy."

He stood up and extended his hand. "I remember you, Mr. Kidd. You used to ask some interesting questions."

He turned to Buddy and extended his hand. Buddy hesitated, as he usually did. He didn't seem to understand why people engage in courtesy rituals. Finally he gave Professor Goodson his dead fish handshake. Goodson turned back to me.

I don't think he yet realized that Buddy was a special case. I had brought him along as part of my program of exposing him to more contacts. He would have rather stayed at home reading his books, but I was determined that he should exercise his limited social skills in the hope of improving them. Buddy was already in his thirties but he looked young for his age and I noticed while we were walking across the campus that, except for his halting walking pace, he looked like a student, maybe not a typical student but one of the studious "nerds" or "geeks."

"Please sit down and tell me what I can do for you," Goodson said.

"Are you familiar with a local company called DataDigm?" I asked as Buddy and I took seats in front of the desk.

"I've heard of it, but I'm afraid I don't know much about it."

"Well, in a nutshell, here is my problem. The founder of the company, Vince Talbot, died and left controlling interest to me. Vince had a Ph.D. in physics and lots of experience in science and engineering as well as several years experience managing a business. I, on the other hand, don't even have a bachelor's degree in anything and zero experience in working at a high tech company. Vince was CEO and Chairman of the Board, and I inherited those positions along with the stock. I'm over my head and was wondering if I could make some kind of arrangement with you for personal consultation."

Dr. Goodson pursed his lips as he looked at me for several seconds. "Well, in the first place I'm surprised that you didn't complete your degree. I would have thought you would have by now since it's been at least a year since you attended one of my classes. Wasn't your major mathematics?"

"I really wasn't working on a degree, but I do have enough hours in math for a bachelor's, maybe even a master's. I have an independent income from oil royalties and so I never planned on a career working for anyone. Not that I'm rich, at least I wasn't until Vince Talbot left me his company. I've been a kind of low grade playboy, I guess. My oil money was just enough to make working unappealing, but gave me only a middle class income."

"So you were here for an education and not for a degree. That's refreshing. I'm more used to students who are here for a degree with the least amount of education required to get it. Well, your lack of a degree may be a loss to society. I remember that your solutions to the examination questions frequently showed an unusual approach. I think you would have made—still could make—a fine scientist."

His words affected me strongly. I guess we all look back at the paths we took in life and wonder about our choices. For a moment I was caught up in what might have been. 'Still could make,' he had said. But I remembered that he had told the class in one of his lectures that most of the really great scientists had done their best work in their twenties, and I was now in my mid thirties.

"I occasionally work as a consultant," he said, breaking the spell. "Did you have in mind solving some particular problem?"

"I was thinking about some kind of arrangement whereby I could drop by your office or perhaps your home and just pick your brain for an hour or so at a time."

He looked puzzled, so I added, "You see, I hate to ask the DataDigm employees too many questions. I'm embarrassed to show my ignorance. They're used to a boss that knows as much or more than they do."

"We can work something like that out, but from our classroom discussions it's hard for me to picture you as being embarrassed to ask questions."

I could see that he wasn't buying the embarrassment line, but I decided to plunge ahead anyway. "If you're free now, I'd like to ask a few questions. You can just send me a statement for your charges or I can have a contract drawn up. Or maybe you can use one of your previous consulting contracts as a model and make it up yourself."

"I'm free right now. Why don't you ask your questions? I must warn you, however, that physics is a very wide field and I don't claim to be expert at everything it includes. It may well be that I can't help you. I don't charge anything for saying, 'I don't know.'"

"Do you know anything about diamond substrates?"

"A little bit. What do you want to know about them?"

"First of all, what are they?"

"A substrate is a layer. A diamond substrate is usually a thin film of diamond. You probably know that diamond is a particular crystal arrangement of pure carbon. Graphite is another form of carbon. Coal is the common form found in nature. The different geometrical arrangements of the atoms make graphite a lubricant and diamond an abrasive. Coal and charcoal are amorphous, which means they do not have a crystalline structure."

"What's a diamond substrate used for?"

"It could be used in different ways. Probably most commonly in making transistors and integrated circuits. A diamond substrate could also serve as a protective skin. I'm sure you know that diamond is the hardest of naturally occurring substances. It has unusual optical properties, highly refractive, and its transparency extends into the ultra violet, making it useful for laser lenses."

He paused for a moment, then continued, "One of the most interesting things about diamond is that it is an electrical insulator but a heat conductor. That's unusual. Most substances that are good heat conductors are also electrical conductors. Diamond is the exception. A thin layer of diamond between layers of conductor makes an excellent capacitor as the diamond can serve as a heat sink as well as a dielectric, an electrical insulator."

"Fine," I said, "you're filling me in on what I need to know. I've been reviewing some work previously done at DataDigm on making diamond substrates. How does that work?"

"As far as I know diamond films are made exclusively by heating carbon—I think usually in the form of graphite—in a vacuum chamber until it vaporizes. When the evaporation chamber is allowed to cool the carbon atoms crystallize as a layer of tiny diamonds."

"Why do they call it an evaporation chamber? I thought they called it *sublimation* when something went from the solid state into the gaseous without first going through a liquid state."

"You're right about sublimation, but carbon does first melt and then evaporate."

Buddy had not said a word since we entered the office, but now he blurted out, "Carbon melts at 3823 Kelvin or 2550 Celsius or 6442 Fahrenheit!"

Professor Buford Goodson jerked his head to stare at Buddy.

"Carbon boils at 4098 Kelvin, or 3825 Celsius or 6917 Fahrenheit. Its atomic number is 6 and its atomic weight is 12.0107. Its density is 2.2670 grams per cubic centimeter."

Goodson turned back to me. "Why did you come to me? Your brother seems to be an expert on carbon."

"Buddy is an autistic-savant. He is someone who knows a lot about trees but doesn't understand the concept of the forest."

Dr. Goodson's glance ping-ponged between Buddy and me, I suppose trying to decide whom to address. He chose Buddy. "Are you a student here?"

Buddy didn't respond so I said, "No, he can't function in a classroom environment. But he reads a lot. In fact he reads constantly, urgently. And his memory is like a sponge."

I paused in case he wanted to talk about Buddy, but he didn't say anything more.

"Back to carbon," I said, "can gemstones be made by this evaporation method?"

"Evidently they can, but I have no knowledge in this area. The trick would be in getting the carbon to grow as a single crystal. I think that the synthetic diamond gemstones on the market are made by this method, but they are engraved by the manufacturer to show that they are man-made."

I felt that I had skillfully guided the conversation into the area of the swamp that I was most interested in, so I waded in further.

"Are these manufactured diamonds facetted by lasers?

"I never heard of that," Goodson said. "I think that the growing process produces a large crystal that is then cut and facetted by expert craftsmen."

"I understand that the synthetics show fluorescence but not the naturals."

"So I understand. I don't know off hand why. The inclusion of tiny graphite regions may be responsible. I don't know."

"If there was a way to keep the manufactured diamond from fluorescing, would there be any other way to tell it from a natural?"

"There might be. Natural diamonds almost always have some impurities, atoms of something other than carbon trapped in the crystal lattice. That's why they come in different colors; the faint color is due to impurities. There are probably impurities present in the manufactured diamonds, too, but not enough to affect the color. Maybe that would be a clue. The impurities in the manu- factured diamonds could be due to something about the chamber in which they are grown, and these might be different from the natural impurities. If the manufactured diamond was made from charcoal or from graphite made from charcoal, it would contain more carbon-14 than the natural stone. Carbon-14 is used in radio-active dating. Its percentage in the air stays constant but once anything dies the carbon-14 gradually changes to carbon-12. Since natural diamond is very old, it could have less 14 than a newly minted one. I'm really just guessing here."

"Carbon-14 has a half-life of 5,730 years," Buddy said.

The professor looked again at Buddy. "Remarkable!"

I wasn't there yet but I felt a little more knowledgeable, closer to what I needed to know.

"I guess that's all the questions for this session. What do I owe you?"

Dr. Goodson smiled. "Oh, I think a lunch would take care of it."

"Just tell me where and when. And maybe you can answer one more question. Why is a natural diamond worth more than a manufactured one?"

"That's easy. Women. I brought roses home the other night to give to my wife. She was thrilled. That is, until I was foolish enough to tell her that I bought them at the grocery store and not at a florist shop. Same thing with diamonds. Give a woman a natural diamond and you're romantic; give her a manufactured diamond and you're cheap."

CHAPTER 33
GO FISH

"My concealed carry permit came in today," Grandpa said over the phone. I was at work still pondering what I should do about the Van Moot situation.

"So did mine."

"Well, why don't we celebrate? The weatherman says tomorrow will be warm and almost calm and I've got an itch to go fishing."

"I don't know, Grandpa. I don't like to be far away from Buddy and Vanessa."

"We'll take them along. We won't go out on one of the big lakes. We'll go to Tyler State Park and have a picnic lunch. After which you and I will wet our hooks for an hour or two while Vanessa and Buddy admire us from the bank. Don't bring your big bass boat. I'll just load my little dingy in my truck and you can have the honor of paddling me around while I teach you how to catch bass."

"You do realize," I said, "that it is illegal to carry firearms into a state park?"

"That's strange. I don't ever remember being searched at the entrance. Don't tell me those Department of Homeland Security boys are going to make us walk through a metal detector and pat us down. Wake up; you live in Texas, not Massachusetts. You're not supposed to take alcoholic beverages, either. That's why they make those foam jackets with soft drink emblems to slip over your beer cans. As long as you behave yourself the Park Rangers don't care."

"I know that. I think the main reason for the firearm ban is to protect the wildlife."

"Well, we're not hunting. We're maybe being hunted. So it don't apply to us."

"Okay, you've won me over. I'll check with Vanessa and if she's willing we'll do it. I'll be out about ten in the morning to help you load the boat."

"Being a smart old man and wise to the ways of the world, I've already checked it out with Vanessa. A man that's not henpecked will lie about other things. I told her Buddy don't like to fish but he seems to enjoy the outdoors. I offered to bring her some tackle, but she says she'd rather just watch and maybe do some reading. She's all for it."

That's how I came to be in a boat with Grandpa the next day out on the small but beautiful lake a few miles north of Tyler. I enjoy fishing anytime of the year but my preferred season for fishing is the fall. Spring is usually too windy, summer is too hot, and winter too cold. In autumn everything falls into place. The heat of the long Texas summer is broken and the south wind begins to slow down as it runs into minor cool fronts moving in from the north. The result is frequent days on a lake where the winds are soft and variable. The shoreline trees complete the setting by streaking the forest with colorful leaves, golden yellow among the sweet gums and bronzy red for the oaks.

But this was early spring, not autumn. Fortunately, there are always a few nice days that crop up in all seasons that seem meant for fishing. On one of those days you were glad you came even if the fish weren't hitting. This was one of those days. The fall colors were long gone but there were white dogwood blossoms among the trees and some blooming redbuds. Most of the other hardwoods still had not slipped green sleeves over their skinny arms, but there were plenty of pines, always green.

Vanessa and Buddy were waiting in her car at the park entrance when Grandpa and I arrived in his truck, and followed us in. We enjoyed a picnic lunch of barbecue sandwiches at one of the camp sites surrounding the lake. There were a few off-season campers, some with tents but most in RVs. There always were, but not enough to spoil the feeling of being away from civilization. We pretty much had the park to ourselves. There was no other boat on the water and nobody was even fishing from the bank or the piers.

Buddy has a built-in dread of water, probably because his poor muscular coordination rules out learning to swim. This keeps him well away from the bank, but he enjoys going out on the piers. They have railings that make it almost impossible to accidently fall in. So he and Vanessa were sitting on one of the peers in folding lawn chairs we had brought for that purpose.

Vanessa had a book and Buddy had about a dozen, and they would look up at us and wave occasionally. I made a point of staying within sight of them. They were on the north side of the lake and we were working the shady south shoreline, but they were easy to spot. Buddy was wearing khaki pants and a white sweat shirt. Vanessa was in jeans and a navy turtle neck looking at this distance with her dark hair like a Ninja warrior.

Grandpa was not an open water man. He liked the backwater regions of lakes, and he often fished the Neches River and other streams away from the rough water of the big lakes. He also had permission to fish in ponds owned by people whom he has known since they were children, and he would take his little boat to those places. Like me, he was a catch-and-release fisherman and so he never depleted his good spots unless the owners specifically asked him to bring them some of his catch. The people who now owned these ponds and small lakes liked and respected Grandpa, but they were not his friends. Their parents or grandparents had been his friends, but most of his generation had passed away.

I suppose that must be the hardest part of growing old. You outlive all your close friends and relatives and new friends are hard to make because the age gap is the greatest of those unseen walls that separate us, stronger than race, sex or wealth, and second only to language. Young people don't have the patience to deal with old people. And vice-versa. But it's more than that. It's a different set of interests and world view, even a different moral code.

Grandpa had said I would paddle him around, and we had a paddle in the boat, but we had put his small electric trolling motor and a deep cycle battery in his truck along with the boat and tackle. My "paddling" was therefore operating the trolling motor, but the soft westerly breeze moved us along the south shore at just the right speed for casting so I only had to touch the trolling motor occasionally to keep us on course.

Like most of Grandpa's possessions, the boat was old and a little battered. It was made of ABS plastic and was blemished in several places where Grandpa had applied patches. It was supposed to be a two-man boat, but we were a little crowded. We had arranged the removable swivel seats as far apart and as close to each end as possible, and our open tackle boxes took up most of the space between us.

We had no trouble loading the boat at Grandpa's and unloading it at the lake. He usually fished alone and I wondered how he was able to handle it by himself.

"How much does this tub weigh, Grandpa?"

"Oh, about a hundred and fifty pounds, I guess"

"Isn't that a little much for you to lift?"

"Well, if you had paid attention to some of those science courses you had in college you'd know that I only have to lift one end at a time. I lift the back end and put it on the tailgate. Then I lift the front end and shove the boat into the truck bed. That's seventy-five pounds for each lift and I can still manage that, as frail and dilapidated as I may seem to you. I use a hand truck to get it to the pickup when I don't have someone with a strong back and a weak mind to help carry it."

Grandpa's tackle box was large and filled with antique lures you might see displayed at a fish hatchery museum or aquarium as relics of a bygone era—big wooden plugs with as many as three sets of triple hooks and once-famous brand names unseen in today's stores. His smallest lures were the size of my largest, and our respective tackle was appropriate to the lures.

I was using light spinning equipment and he held a heavier rod containing a bait casting reel. My line was rated at four pounds and his at twelve. Grandpa loved top water lures and was dropping them accurately into likely looking shady spots and working them slowly, so far without success. I had just unhooked and released my second bass.

Grandpa was wearing a black baseball cap with the legend "Wildcats" on the front, referring to a team that went out of business about thirty years ago. "What do you call that thing you're using for bait?" he said.

"This is what's known by us experts as a wacky worm. It's a soft plastic worm hooked in the middle instead of the end and cast without any additional weight except the hook. The color is watermelon red. I'd be glad to lend you one if you think you can cast it with that salt water marlin tackle you're using. I don't have but a dozen or so and I doubt they'd be heavy enough for you to cast if you put them all on your hook at the same time."

Grandpa took off his top water lure and started rummaging through his tackle box. "If you were to hook a real bass he'd take that skinny little rod away from you and beat you with it."

"Seriously, Grandpa, you could cast it if you put a little sinker about a foot ahead of the hook. Want to try it?"

"I never liked those plastic worms. The fish gum around on them. If you set the hook too soon you tear the hook off the worm and if you're too slow they spit it out or swallow it so that you can't get the hook out without killing them."

He was right about that, and it had taken a lot of experience to teach me exactly when to set the hook. He took out a jar and unscrewed the lid. "Now here is a bass killer that's so effective that it's outlawed to all but a small group of certified experts who are sworn to release their catch. It was enticing bass long before plastic worms were invented and will still be doing so after the plastic worm fad fades away. It is the dreaded pork rind frog, made from the hide of a real hog and heavy enough to cast with a manly rod and line."

The soft plastic worm "fad" had been going on for about fifty years. He removed the bait from its little jar of salt water, ran a 2/0 hook through it and tied it to his line. As he began casting I took a look at the pier on the opposite side of the lake where Vanessa and Buddy were still relaxing in their chairs. I watched until Vanessa looked up. Then I waved. Vanessa waved back.

Grandpa retrieved the frog imposter with frequent small jerks and the little legs moved in a kicking motion as if they were the source of the frog's movement. On his third cast he got a good strike and set the hook. It wasn't a huge bass, about a three-pounder, but larger than either of the two I had caught. Grandpa brought him in close to the boat and I got the landing net ready.

"No need for that when you use fishing line instead of spider web," he said as he took hold of the line about a foot ahead of the fish and simply lifted him into the boat. When he unhooked the bass, he held it up for Vanessa and Buddy to behold. I turned to get their reaction.

They were gone.

CHAPTER 34
A WALK IN THE PARK

Ordinarily Grandpa would have gently placed the bass in the water and given it a kindly nudge to get it swimming and then he would have rinsed his hands in the lake water. This time he simply tossed it as you would a wad of paper toward the trash basket. He didn't even look to see where it landed.

I was already turning on the electric trolling motor and revving it up to maximum speed as I headed the boat for the pier across the lake. About three miles per hour was all I could get out of it, but we were only a little over a football field's length from the pier when we started. I picked up the paddle, our backup power source, and added some powerful strokes to the force of the little electric motor. This almost doubled our speed, but it seemed to take forever to cross that stretch of water.

"Watch your head, Grandpa," I shouted as we approached the pier.

I lay the paddle in the boat and shut off the motor just as the bow of the boat passed between two of the pilings supporting the pier. I stood up and grabbed the deck and pulled myself up as the boat plowed on under the structure. I clambered over the railing.

The lawn chairs and books were still there but there was no sign of Buddy and Vanessa. I ran up the pier to the bank, where a trail led up to the picnic area where we had lunched. I ran up the hill past the picnic table we had used. At the top of the hill I saw Vanessa and Buddy hugging each other. A large man was walking away toward the parking area. A dirty and somewhat battered black Ford pickup was the only vehicle besides ours there.

When I reached them I could hear Buddy crying and Vanessa trying to comfort him. She looked up as I touched them.

"Who?" I said.

"Him," she said. Pointing to the man that I had seen. "He . . ."

I didn't wait for the explanation. I sprinted after him. He didn't hear me until I was almost on him, and I plowed into him as he turned. He felt the impact of my shoulder in his gut, and when we went down together he felt the impact of the ground more because he was on the bottom. I got up first and set my feet, waiting for him. He was a big man, taller and heavier than me. His muscles bulged. He had that pumped up look common to newly released felons who had no entertainment in prison except lifting weights. While he was getting to his feet I looked around. There were no campers or rangers within sight. Good.

During my hitch in the Marine Corps I had been picked because of my boxing skill to first learn and then instruct in hand-to-hand combat. I wasn't in as good a shape now—I was feeling the effect of climbing onto the pier and scrambling up the hill—but my breathing was getting easier and I was calm and ready. The big guy came reaching at me without saying a word and I had him back on the ground in no time.

He was a little slower getting up this time. Before he made a move toward me he said, "What's this about?"

"You tell me," I said.

He came at me again, this time he tried to box instead of grapple. I liked that better. I'll have to give him credit for being tough. His face was marked up pretty well by the time he went down for the third time. I hadn't neglected his abdomen and kidneys, either.

This time he stopped before he got all the way up. He still had one knee on the ground when he said, "I don't even know you."

"I know you, though. I've known you all my life. You took lunch money from the smaller kids in grade school. You like to make people cry."

By this time Vanessa and Buddy had come up to us.

"He seemed friendly at first," Vanessa said, "But he kept picking on Buddy. He said he was going to throw him in the water. That's when I took Buddy off the pier and started back to the car. But he followed us. He kept asking Buddy if he wanted a swimming lesson."

"I was only joking," he said as he completed his rise to his feet. "I got nothing against retards."

I caught him with a hard left hook to the chin and he was down again. As he lay on his stomach I took his billfold from his hip pocket. I thought he was out, but he rolled over on his side. "Hey! That's my billfold. You can't rob me."

"I'll return it in just a second," I said. I opened it and took his driver's license out and handed it to Buddy. Buddy had stopped sniffling and was watching the events with interest. "Memorize the name, address, and everything else on this card, Buddy."

Buddy read aloud everything on the license, including the date of birth and the license number. Then he handed it back to me. I knew he had stored all that in his brain and we could write it down later.

I looked at the name on the card, "All right, Mr. Eugene Willis Carlton, I've got your name and address. Now you better take a good look at my brother and this woman and hope to God that nothing mysterious happens to them in the future. Because if it does I'm going to look you up and beat you to death. That's not a figure of speech. I will beat you until you are dead. When you go down you'll never get up. That's when the kicking and stomping start."

I threw the billfold and the license card at him, and we walked back to the peer to see what had happened to Grandpa. He met us on the trail before we got to the peer. He was well and sound but he was wet from the knees down because of his rush to get out of the boat and catch up with me.

"Do you think he was connected to this Van Loon thing?" he said. I don't know why Grandpa had so much trouble saying Van Moot.

"I'm not sure. I think Van Moot would hire a higher type of hoodlum, but Buddy knows how to find him if we need to."

"Did you recognize him? Was he one of those gangsters that we ran into before?"

"I don't remember ever seeing him before," I said. "He may just be an old- fashioned bully. He was pumped up physically like a newly released felon. Our penal system believes in getting the muggers in top shape to resume their trade immediately on release. At any rate, if I see him again I've got his number."

"I've got his number," Buddy said. Then he recited it.

CHAPTER 35
GOING DUTCH

Vanessa's house was technically still Vince's house and would be so until Thomas Jackson had done the necessary legal work to transfer ownership. It was now headquarters for Vanessa, me, Buddy, and Grandpa until we were all out of danger. I liked to think that I was the only one truly in danger, but I wasn't sure that those I loved wouldn't be used to get to me. We all slept there, but Grandpa refused to spend as much time in the house as I would have liked.

He slept there and was usually with us for the evening meal but he was an early riser and would make coffee and scramble an egg for himself before the rest of us were up. Then he would drive his pickup back to his farm and spend most of the day there.

He still called his place a farm although cattle were now his main crop. Most of the old East Texas farms were now devoted to raising cattle. The younger rural land owners called their places ranches even though the acreage was tiny compared to the ranches of south and west Texas. Whichever term was more accurate, *ranch* had more romance to it for the newer generation than *cattle farm*.

Buddy had surprised me by adjusting quickly to his new surroundings. I had feared that he would miss our small house and his routine there. I think that Vince's extensive library held a charm for him that made the transition easier. In fact, I was beginning to worry whether he would ever want to move back to our own small house. I think he had fallen in love with Vanessa, not in the sexual sense—he seemed to lack any sexual drive at all—but he seemed to enjoy her presence. And she was wonderful with him, treating him as an equal and not ordering him around at all, and yet managing him without seeming to be bossy.

Dinner (*supper* to Grandpa) was the meal when we usually were all together. Since I was now often eating out for lunch in order to get to know the DataDigm employees better, dinner was when we put our heads together to plan strategy. I wanted to take Vanessa out more often, but she was having too much fun playing gourmet cook. She had put in a stock of wines and was experimenting with which kinds went best with the particular main course she prepared, which tonight was shrimp fried rice.

"This is some recipe," I said after taking a few forkfuls. "You're turning out to be quite the chef."

"I hate to have to confess, but tonight you are eating pre-prepared food. This is just made by dumping one of the frozen packages from the grocery store into the skillet."

"Well, I don't believe it. Buddy and I have eaten shrimp fried rice made that way before, and it never tasted this good."

Vanessa smiled. "The secret is to buy frozen shrimp separately. Then you add them to the skillet until you have about three of four times as many as come in the package."

"Aha!" said Grandpa, "I always said that those frozen shrimp dishes were bad for your eyes. You strain them looking for the shrimp."

"The big question tonight is which wine goes best with shrimp fried rice, that is, which of the three I've set out. There's Chablis, Sauterne and Rhine wine. Please try a little of each and let me know your preference."

"At my house," Grandpa said, "I keep only one kind of alcoholic drink, vodka. I use the cheapest brand I can find because I can't tell the difference between the cheapest and the most expensive and neither can my guests. When I have company I ask them what they want to drink. If they say vodka, I've got them covered. If they say gin, I add a drop of juniper juice. If they say scotch, I pour in a little barbecue sauce to give it color and a smoky flavor. If they say white wine, I just dilute the vodka with water. If they say red wine, I color it with grape juice. If they want champagne, I add an Alka-Seltzer. Nobody ever notices."

As I mentioned previously, Grandpa is good at deadpan, so Vanessa studied Grandpa's poker face a moment before she laughed and said,

"Tom, your vote won't count in the wine tasting tonight."

"Grandpa, exactly where do you buy juniper juice?" I said. "I don't ever remember seeing a bottle at your house. In fact, I don't recall ever seeing any for sale at the grocery store, either."

"Well, smarty, I've been told that what we call cedar trees here in Texas are really junipers, the true cedar being an old world plant. I keep a few berries from my own trees in the pantry to squeeze for my gin drinking friends. If they ain't juniper, then that shows how ignorant gin drinkers are 'cause they never notice the difference."

Vanessa always treated Buddy as if he were normal and asked his opinion on both the main course and the wine. Buddy is always as honest as a child. "It's all right. Not as good as hamburger or chicken fried steak. The wine tastes bad. Can I have some Dr. Pepper?"

Vanessa smiled and went to the refrigerator for the soft drink. I saw that it was Coke she filled the glass with, but Buddy didn't notice the difference. Maybe Grandpa is on to something.

After dinner Buddy went into the library while the rest of us stayed at the table. Grandpa and Vanessa looked at me. They seemed to think I had some news or a new plan to reveal. I didn't but felt I needed to say something that sounded like a plan.

"Well," I said, "there are two ways to go with this thing. One, I can contact Van Moot and give him the full story along with the flash drive. And I can tell him my suspicion that someone at DataDigm has used Vince's equipment to manufacture some more diamonds. Two, I can wait until I can pin down who that person is and hand him over along with the flash drive."

"I like Plan One best," Grandpa said. "You may never get the goods on the person that made the new stones. The first way is something you can do right away. Let's get done with it. When you deliver that gadget you'll have done everything Vince Talbot asked you to do. If Van Loon don't like it he'll have to lump it. If he wants you to solve all his problems for him, well, that's just too much sugar for a dime."

I looked at Vanessa, and she nodded. "Tom's right. If that doesn't satisfy Van Moot we still won't be any worse off than we are now. If it does satisfy him, then it's over. Why do you think you need to catch the DataDigm person? Let Van Moot do that."

I knew they were right, but there was something else involved. Suppose it wasn't the diamond cartel that had been trailing me? Suppose it was the maker of the Dallas diamond. Then it had to be someone at DataDigm who had threatened me, assaulted me, insulted me. He had wrecked my pickup and put me in the hospital. I still had aches and bruise marks. And he had endangered the only three people I cared much about. And that same person had betrayed

Vince Talbot, the best friend I ever had. That person was going to pay.

"All right," I said. "Tomorrow I will try to contact Van Moot. That's plan A. But I'm also going to put Plan B into operation. I'm going to track down the bastard that got us into this mess."

CHAPTER 36
FLYING DUTCHMAN

I got to the office early the next morning. The security guard had turned off the alarm and unlocked the front door, but I was one of the first to come inside. There were two items on my agenda for the day. The first was to contact Van Moot. The second was to get into the storage room where I thought Vince's diamond producing machine might be located.

Van Moot wasn't in but his secretary was. I left her the message that I had found something that belonged to him and would be glad to give it to him. He was to tell me how it should be delivered. She said she would have him call me when he got in. The ball was now in Van Moot's court, so I turned to the next item on the agenda, the storage room.

I walked to Carl's office. He wasn't there so I moved on to Jack McKinney's. Jack came in right after me. It was still before official starting time, although DataDigm didn't enforce strict hours.

"What's up?" Jack said.

"If you have that combination to the storage room, I'd like to get it from you. Or would you like to come along and explain things?"

"I'd like to come along. The only thing is I still haven't heard from Carl what the combination is."

Damn! I was beginning to feel sure I was getting the run around. "Carl's not here yet," I said. "Would you mind keeping an eye out for him and getting back to me when you get the combination?"

"Sure thing."

I went to the office door and opened it. I decided to leave it open at least until I heard from either Carl or Jack McKinney. When I seated myself again behind my desk, I found that I had a good view of hall traffic. Maybe I would make that my policy, an "open door policy" making me more accessible and at the same time more aware of what was going on. I wondered if Vince had kept the door closed or open.

About 11 o'clock Jack McKinney came to the threshold. I waved him in.

"Well," he said as he approached the desk, "I got a new combination from Carl, but I still can't get the lock to work. Neither can Carl. You're supposed to be able to reset the combination in a case like this, but Carl can't make that work, either. He says he'll get it open tomorrow for sure if he has to call in a locksmith."

I didn't know whether it was Carl or Jack, but by now I was sure somebody was stalling me. I tried to keep annoyance out of my voice. "Tell Carl never mind about the locksmith. I'll have one of our machine shop guys open it first thing in the morning. Tell Carl to fix it so that opening that door won't set off any alarms."

I watched Jack for reactions. If my words had given him any cause for worry he didn't show it at all. "Okay, I'll pass the word to Carl. I'm sure they can disconnect individual doors from the general alarm system just for cases like this. No use having a room if nobody can get in. Let me know when you get it open if you want me to explain any of the equipment in there."

I nodded in what I hoped was a casual manner. "I don't think there's anything important in there. It's just that I'm tired of being frustrated by this lock business. I'm sure any of the guys in the machine shop could open that door. Which machinist would do it with the least damage to the door?"

"I'd use Bob Berman. He's about the best at anything."

I'd met Bob. In fact, by this time I'd met just about everyone at DataDigm. I had been impressed by Berman, a short portly man with a narrow mustache who wore bib overalls instead of the white work clothes the company provided the technicians. He may have looked like a farmer but he seemed familiar with the most advanced techniques of prototype manufacture. "Would you mind asking him to meet me at the door at nine tomorrow morning?"

"We could do it right now, if you like."

Jack surprised me with that. I was tempted to say yes. His readiness seemed to eliminate him as the source of the delays I'd been getting. But if I agreed, would Jack come back with some excuse? I didn't want in that room today because I was making plans for tonight.

What I wanted was for everyone to know that if something was to be removed from the storage room it would have to be done tonight. "No, I've got other stuff to take care of today. Nine tomorrow should give Carl time to do whatever needs to be done about the alarm. There's no hurry. It's like you said, what's the use of having a room nobody can get into?"

I had lunch with Vanessa and Buddy at her house. She looked so attractive in blue jeans and white T-shirt striped red, black, and blue that I almost decided to take the afternoon off. But I needed to be available at the office for Van Moot's telephone call, assuming he would return mine. Vanessa had prepared beef Stroganoff, this time from scratch, and it was delicious. I wondered if her new-found interest in cooking would be temporary or if, now that she had no reason for a job, she had found gourmet cooking as a substitute for a working career.

Buddy liked the Stroganoff, I think principally because the steak was already cut into bite-size pieces. Vanessa had taken him with her grocery shopping. She said he was no trouble except he tended to linger reading the box labels and reciting them later. "I'd be picking up stuff while he was reciting ingredients and cooking directions for items we had passed two rows back.

It was a little distracting. But I've put that talent to good use when I cook. I read the recipe and instructions to Buddy. Then I have him hang around while I prepare things. Instead of going back and forth to the cookbook, I ask Buddy what I do after I blend in the sour cream or whatever, and he tells me. We make a great team."

"We're a team," Buddy said.

"Right, Buddy," I said. "You and Vanessa prepare the food and I play my part in the team by eating it."

Back at the office I kept expecting Van Moot to call. Waiting for an important call just about kills my ability to do anything else, so I wasn't accomplishing much. A little after four, Antoinette buzzed me. "Mr. Van Moot is here to see you."

"Show him in." How could that be? I did a little calculating and decided it was conceivable that Van Moot could have taken a private jet and gotten here by now. But it seemed more logical that he hadn't been in the New York office at all when I called. He could have been much closer, at one of their branch offices in, say, Dallas. Or he could have been right here in Tyler, Texas, all the time.

When Van Moot entered my office he got right to the point. "I got your message and flew right out. What is it you have to give me?"

I had at that time two flash drives on my person. A decoy in my trousers pocket and the critical one in a little bag pinned to the inside of my trousers at waist level. Van Moot stared while I undid my belt and opened the front of my trousers. I don't know what he expected but he remained silent and expressionless while I unpinned the bag and laid it on the desk. After I zipped up and refastened my belt, I opened the bag and handed Van Moot the flash drive.

"As far as I'm concerned," I said, "this ends my obligation to you and those you represent."

"It does providing, of course, this is the authentic device and it contains what Mr. Talbot promised. And it has not been duplicated."

"It does regardless of anything. I have done everything Vince Talbot charged me with doing in regard to this matter. My responsibility has been fulfilled. And please notice that I voluntarily gave you the flash drive without your having to drive me into a ditch and take it off my unconscious body."

"There is still the matter of someone using Mr. Talbot's methods, which were supposed to be kept secret."

"Sit down, Mr. Van Moot," I said as I sat down myself behind the desk. "Let's stop pussy footing around and say what we mean. Vince figured out a way to make synthetic diamonds that were practically impossible to tell from mined diamonds. He built a device that would turn them out fully faceted as if cut by an expert. I don't know how his device worked and I don't care. Rather than go into the business of fabricating diamonds he sold the knowledge of how to do it to you and your cronies. For reasons I don't fully understand you elected to pay him by channeling contracts to him from various companies that your outfit controls. Are we together so far?"

"The situation is roughly as you describe it. Please continue."

"Maybe Vince was planning to make things simpler for me and died before he could complete his plans. I don't know. He left me a locked briefcase and note to destroy it without opening it. I did that. When we first talked I thought that I had already done my part in its entirety. Later I discovered that Vince had left a flash drive to be delivered to you. I have now done that. I have not opened the flash drive, mainly because I presumed that doing so would mark it in some way that you would know it had been opened. I don't want to leave you with the suspicion that I am capable of or interested in reviving Vince's device."

"A wise decision."

"And that's another thing. You have a way of suggesting veiled threats, which you just did. I don't like it. Since I met you I have been physically assaulted and have been driven off the road and put into the hospital with a concussion. Now I'm telling you that the next time you have someone attack me he better not screw up because I will be coming after you and I won't screw up. And no matter how big your cartel may be, it can't protect you from a trained sniper that can kill you from half a mile away."

"Well, no one would accuse you of veiling your threats. As to the assaults, I knew of the one in which you were forced off the road. I know nothing about the other. I had nothing to do with either."

"Do you mean to say that you had nothing to do with the four thugs that confronted me and my grandfather and my brother and tried to force me into their car at gun point?"

"Nothing whatsoever. I wasn't even aware such a thing had taken place."

"What about the burglarizing of Vince's house?"

"I am aware of it but had nothing to do with it."

"Do you know who is responsible?"

"No.

"Care to make a guess?"

"No. Guessing is not in my line."

"Well let's see if we can figure it out. You have implied that someone has sold or tried to sell a large diamond since Vince's death. Is that right?"

"Yes, and that is why I said you had failed in your responsibility to protect Talbot's invention."

"And you base your conclusion that that gem was made by Vince's method because of the unusual, antiquated cut of the stone?"

"Yes, precisely. Mr. Talbot had a small store of his manufactured gems and it could have come from there. He didn't make the sale himself. He was dead at the time of the sale. The stone was manufactured and not an antique. We know that because, although Talbot diamonds pass the usual tests, other more sophisticated tests pin the diamond to his process. That points to you. You could have inherited Talbot's small stash or could have learned the process and produced a new gem."

I started to tell him about finding Vince's velvet bag full of diamonds, but thought better of it. That would have made him suspect me all the more as the one who had made the sale. "I didn't do it. Let's operate on the assumption that both of us are telling the truth. Then a third person is involved. My theory is that someone at DataDigm figured out what Vince had done and revived the scrapped device Vince had used. But as last configured the device could make only the antiquated facet design that was only one of Vince's patterns. That individual therefore manufactured one or more large gems and sold at least one of them."

"If it is not you, then you offer a plausible explanation. But you won't be off the hook until you identify that individual."

"I'm already off the hook, as I told you. I've done everything Vince asked me to do. Come after me and I will go after you."

Van Moot pursed his lip, started to say something, and then fell silent.

"However," I said, "I will do something for you above and beyond the call of duty. I will try to put this unknown individual into your hands. Are you available tonight from about ten o'clock until dawn?"

CHAPTER 37
DEER BLIND

At the evening gathering at Vanessa's the four of us were sitting around the dining room table as had become our custom. Vanessa had prepared stuffed fillet of sole with some sort of fancy dressing. She was becoming more confident about wine and didn't give us a choice. It was Riesling tonight, and it seemed to me to be perfect for the meal. If the way to a man's heart is through his stomach, she had me. Grandpa made a joke about "soul" food and went after it with gusto. Buddy is usually pretty much indifferent about food, but seemed to eat a little more enthusiastically after Vanessa said, "Buddy helped me fix dinner."

"I'm going out after a while," I said. "I'll be gone all night."

Even Buddy added his stare to the four other eyes suddenly turned on me.

"If anyone calls for me while I'm gone, take a message and tell them I'll be back in a little while."

"What's up?" Grandpa said.

"Well, I've sort of laid a trap and I've got to watch it all night to see if anyone comes to the bait."

Vanessa raised her eyebrows. It was clear she wanted more details.

"I'm assuming," I said, "that someone has resurrected Vince's device and has used it to make at least one diamond. I further assume that the device is still at DataDigm. If it is, then by the process of elimination, it must be in a certain storage room. The door to that room has a lock that doesn't respond to its supposed combination. This morning I put out the word that tomorrow morning I'm going to have that lock removed, the door opened, and the room inspected. I'm sure everyone in the company knows about that by now. That means that the person I'm looking for will have to come tonight and remove Vince's device. I'll be waiting for him."

Grandpa was the first to respond. "Okay, this is where I come in. You're going to need backup."

"I don't want to cut you out, Grandpa, but a certain man named Van Moot has already taken that job. Besides, Vanessa and Buddy ought not to be left alone."

"My God! If that Van Loon is going to sit up with you, you sure as hell need me to keep an eye on him."

I looked at Grandpa. *Old man, if I caused something to happened to you I could never forgive myself.* I started to tell Grandpa how important it was for him to stay and guard Vanessa and Buddy—it was plausible and should keep him safe.

Then I saw the excitement in his eyes. It must be hell to be restricted by age, people constantly discounting your ability to be useful—no excitement, too old to work, too old to participate, friends all dead or incapacitated, and no one wanting to be a new friend to an aging person. "You're absolutely right. I'll need you to watch my back."

Vanessa looked at me in surprise. Then I saw her expression change as if she were reading my thoughts. "Buddy and I will be all right, Tom. Don't worry about us. You go where you're most needed."

Grandpa and I were both armed when we left Vanessa's and even more heavily armed when we left my house. We'd stopped there for me to change into blue jeans and jacket and to pick up my Model 700 Remington 30-'06 deer rifle. Its big telescope sight could gather enough light to shoot almost in the dark. I hadn't been deer hunting in years, but I had taken it to the range last fall and knew that the sights were still dead on. I had two pairs of good binoculars also, one for each of us. I brewed coffee and put it into a thermos bottle. I started to fill a second thermos with coffee but Grandpa shook his head.

"I'll just borrow one of your canteens," he said. "When it comes to slaughter you will do your work on water." Kipling had always been Grandpa's favorite poet.

It was only a little after eight o'clock when Grandpa and I got to DataDigm. The company property was on the outskirts of Tyler and no one had yet built next to it. The parking lot was lighted but there was no external security devices except for spot lights trained on the building. The fence at the gate covered only the front of the property and did not extend to the sides or back. The building faced east and I let Grandpa with the rifle out at the north front corner of the property line.

We had gone over my hand-drawn map and Grandpa knew exactly where his assigned station was. The night watchman would be making rounds inside the building periodically and recording the times at which he checked various locked doors. Between rounds he could be anywhere within the building but would most likely be seated in Antoinette's chair in the front vestibule. He was not required to go outside at any time, but could if he saw a need to. So long as Grandpa kept away from the main building, he should not have to worry about being seen.

"Remember," I said in a low voice—whispering didn't work well with Grandpa even when he was wearing his hearing aids, which he now was— "There may be three of us. Van Moot may have someone with him or may insist on bringing someone from law enforcement."

Grandpa nodded as he slipped out of the front passenger seat and quietly opened the back door. It had been a pleasant spring day but was now growing cooler and Grandpa knew that it would get downright chilly before dawn so he picked up one of the blankets and a small pillow from the pile of things I had stowed there. He stole away in the stooped mode of a hunter, keeping a low silhouette.

I thought of his stories about poaching. He never broke any laws that I knew of except poaching laws. He called it guest hunting. "I *guessed* nobody was watching so I stepped over the fence," he would say. There are plenty of deer in East Texas today, but back in those days East Texas was all farming, not ranching, country and farmers kept the deer killed out to protect their crops. So he and his pals would pool to buy a deer lease in the Hill Country of central Texas. Often the ranch they leased would be poor hunting compared to one adjacent to it. "Guest hunting" was too tempting for Grandpa to resist and I think the danger of being caught added zest to it. The result was that he had considerable practice in skulking and hiding from both game and gamekeepers.

After leaving Grandpa I headed for Van Moot's hotel. I had been a little surprised when Van Moot had agreed to tonight's adventure. I had him figured for someone who delegated the dirty work. Now I wondered if he had been the driver of the car the three hoods got out of to accost Grandpa, Buddy, and me. The driver was the only one I didn't get a good look at. Of course, Van Moot denied any connection to that event and I was more or less taking him at his word, at least for tonight. But only more or less.

Van Moot's hotel was on the opposite, east, side of the city, several miles from DataDigm.

When I knocked on his door I wasn't surprised when it was opened by a man in his thirties, tall and well built. "This is Mr. Holt," Van Moot said. "He's accompanying us on this little adventure. Ernest, this is Michael Kidd."

We shook hands and Holt applied just slightly more pressure than was called for to let me know he was tough. Both of them were dressed in business suits. I guess they hadn't brought anything else with them. Van Moot must have paid at least a thousand dollars for the perfectly tailored suit he had on. *If it gets ruined I guess he can afford it.*

"Okay," I said, "let's get on the road."

Without further conversation they followed me to the Avalon and we got in, Van Moot and I up front and Holt in the back seat. No one said a word on the way to DataDigm. As we passed in front of the entrance drive, I slowed down. "I can let you out here," I said to Van Moot. "Or you can stay in the car and walk back with me. About 200 yards up this road there's an intersection with a little dirt road. I'm going to park there and walk back."

"We'll stay with you."

So the three of us walked back to the plant entrance drive and then more stealthily approached the main building. It was 10:34 by my watch. I was carrying a thermos of coffee and three boat cushions. Holt was lugging some blankets. I had loaded Van Moot down with three Styrofoam cups. I'm sure he realized that I had

245

correctly anticipated his bringing his body guard, or whatever he called Holt.

We skirted the parking lot, walking around it on the south side. We stayed well out of the lights that played on the parking lot. I saw exactly four cars, one I recognized as Martin Spencer's and one must have belonged to the night watchman, and I could see him moving around in the entry vestibule. There was a well-kept lawn around the whole complex.

I led my guests to a spot I had selected earlier that day. Bushes would hide us from the parking lot and we had a clear view of the back loading bays. Over the top of the bushes we could also watch the parking lot. I scanned the darkness behind the building but couldn't see a sign of Grandpa. I hadn't expected to and would have been disappointed if I had.

I placed the three boat cushions on the ground. "Have you fellows ever done any big game hunting?"

Van Moot shook his head, but Holt said, "A little."

"Well, this is like hunting from a deer blind. You stay quiet and move as little as possible and watch for the deer to come. The key thing is to see without being seen."

Holt removed a pistol from its shoulder holster and studied it. "You use rifles for deer hunting."

"In this case," I said, "we want to take the deer alive. Please remember that."

"Yes," Van Moot said, "we don't want anyone killed here tonight. You are not to use that weapon unless you have to in order to save your life or my own."

"Or mine?" I asked.

"Of course," Van Moot added. "Or yours."

CHAPTER 38
MIDNIGHT CALLER

By 11 o'clock all the cars in the lot had pulled out except for the night watchman's and Martin Spencer's. Looking at Martin's heap made me realize how practical he was. It was a reliable means of transportation; that's all he cared about. He was indifferent to what others thought about him or his car.

I again thought of a possible connection between genius and autism, at least some forms of autism. Both Buddy and Martin could do almost incredible things with their brains, and both were inept at social contact. Of course, Martin was much better socially than Buddy, but that was only a matter of degree. They were both more interested in things or ideas than they were in people. Buddy just didn't make any effort to disguise his lack of interest whereas Martin felt enough peer pressure to make a meager effort at being polite if not sociable. I wondered if Buddy would have been another useful genius if only some errant gene had not been defective.

I visualized Martin as working on some computer-related problem and losing track of time. He would eventually look at his watch and be amazed at how late it had become. Or, more likely, he would eventually be brought back to reality by a seizure of hunger pangs.

We had been at our station only a little over an hour when my companions began to show signs of impatience. Van Moot began to shift his body position at short intervals. Holt spread his blanket on the ground and lay down on it facing the starry sky. I didn't scold them for making unnecessary movements because I didn't think there was any danger of our being seen from within the building.

Those hunger pangs must have hit Martin about midnight. That's when he appeared in the parking lot heading for his car. He got in, started the car and pulled out down the drive. Now only the night watchman's car was in place.

"Suppose nobody comes," Holt said.

"Then we've wasted a night," I said.

"Do you suspect a particular individual?" Van Moot asked.

"Yes, but I'd rather not name names without more evidence. There should be two people together in one car. I figure the most likely time to be about one in the morning, but anytime between now and dawn is possible. If nobody shows up by about five, I'd say we can write it off as my mistake."

The floodlights surrounding the building made it stand out starkly against the black sky. The back corner we were facing showed two conflicting architectural styles. The back of the building was box-like and ugly, testifying to the simple utilitarian steel structure that was the reality behind the stone veneer that faced the front and the parking lot.

The only sound was a chorus of frogs suggesting that a creek was not far off. By one o'clock both Van Moot and Holt were wrapped in blankets. Sitting on their cushions and hunched over, they made me think of Indians waiting stoically for something to happen. A little before one-thirty something did happen.

The headlights of a car appeared in the drive. I didn't recognize the car as belonging to anyone I knew. It was one of those Chryslers that look like a smaller version of the gangster cars seen in movies about the 1930s, black or dark blue. I was expecting something larger, a van or SUV, but I had no clear mental picture of the size of Vince's device and maybe it was smaller than I had imagined.

The car didn't park close to the front door, but toward us, well around the corner out of sight of anyone in the entrance vestibule. The car lights went out and a man got out and walked toward the entrance, passing out of our line of sight. I couldn't be sure of his identity at that distance. Then the car started up again and, without turning on the headlights, moved around in front of us and pulled into one of the loading bays, the one connected to the junkyard room. We were in business.

Van Moot and Holt came out of their blankets and were straining to see, their eyes on the loading door. It was only about as wide as an ordinary single car garage door, but raising it would make some noise.

The man from the Chrysler would have to time his actions precisely. The watchman would have to be in another part of the building. I figured that our man would stall around in the junkyard until the watchman showed up on his rounds. When the watchman left, he would allow so many minutes and then raise the door. A leisurely walk around the building checking locks would take about twenty minutes, and if our man allowed five minutes after the watchman left him, that would mean we would have to wait for a maximum of twenty-five minutes before the door opened.

My two guests simultaneously turned and looked at me. "It will be a few minutes," I whispered, glancing at my watch.

I looked again toward the spot where I had told Grandpa to take. I could see no sign of him but that was all right, I didn't expect to see him. I knew he would be looking intently at the back door the same as we were. Whoever was driving the Chrysler stayed in the car, and I couldn't see well enough to recognize anyone even with the binoculars. We were all like statues for about ten minutes. Then the loading door slid upward in its tracks, and a man appeared in silhouette against the lighted interior.

The driver of the Chrysler got out and hurried up the loading dock steps. It was a woman. The man moved out of sight for a moment and then reappeared with a hand truck bearing something angular.

Had they come in a truck it would have been a simple matter to back up to the dock and wheel the object on board. But their car was much too low for that so they were compelled to take it down the steps, letting the hand truck slide one step at a time the woman leading and steadying the load while the man pulled back to let it slide gently to the next step. When they were about half way to the ground I rose and moved slowly toward them, my two companions followed.

The two thieves were concentrating on their work and they did not see us until we were standing at the rear of the car. At just that time the hand truck reached ground level and they straightened up and looked around. They saw us immediately.

"Carl," I said, "I believe you know Mr. Van Moot. Antoinette, you remember him, I'm sure. This other gentleman is Ernest Holt, his assistant."

They stared like animals caught in auto headlights. The woman was Antoinette Black.

"Yes," Carl said at last, "I've met Mr. Van Moot."

"I see you couldn't wait for nine o'clock to open the storage room."

"No."

"Of course, you didn't need a locksmith. There was nothing the matter with the lock in the first place. You changed the combination without telling anyone. I take it that is Vince's diamond-making device?"

No answer. I turned to Van Moot. "The next step is yours. This device belongs to you according to your agreement with Vince Talbot. You can take delivery of this device now and call it a day, or you can use your cell phone to call the police and charge Carl and Antoinette with theft. It's up to you."

Van Moot hesitated. I turned to Holt and held out my car keys. "While your boss is making up his mind, I suggest that you bring my car around here so we can load this thing in it."

Holt looked at Van Moot, who nodded. Holt started at a dog trot for the Avalon.

"Of course," Van Moot said, "if we let him go we'll never know how many diamonds this man made."

"Two!" Carl said. "One I sold in Dallas. You can have the other one."

Van Moot shrugged. "But how can I believe you?"

"However many he made were in the antiquated facet design. I take it you can make it difficult to sell that design. That's why he kept trying to find out how to change the design. That's what he thought he could scare or beat out of me."

Van Moot nodded. "Yes, we will be informed whenever such a stone appears in the future, and we will track down the seller."

There goes my own little diamond nest egg. Oh well, I still had the smaller diamonds, and maybe I could find someone to re-cut the big ones. I'd have to talk with Jean Hebert.

It all seemed a bit anticlimactic. Here we were, all polite and civilized, concluding an adventure filled with violence and threats of yet more violence. Carl would be out of a job, of course, but Van Moot probably wasn't going to prefer charges because of the bad publicity it would give to the diamond industry. The more publicity given to man-made diamonds the shakier the mystique of the mined stones would become.

The rage I had felt against an unknown foe who threatened me and my loved ones seemed to disappear now that my enemy was revealed as a rather ordinary guy who had let dreams of wealth blur his perception of decent behavior. I was not going to prefer charges, either. He did owe me for repairs or a new truck, and I would ask for that.

"Where is the second diamond that you made?" Van Moot said.

"I have it right here, and you're welcome to it," Carl said.

He reached into his outside coat pocket, fumbled a second, and brought out a small revolver. He fired one shot into Van Moot, who folded forward and sank to his knees.

CHAPTER 39
THE DEAL

My mind was racing simultaneously along different tracks. I thought about Ernest Holt; he should be about half-way to my car when he heard the shot. He would be torn between going on for the car or heading back on the run. Either way he wouldn't get here in time to prevent Carl from getting off another shot, or several shots for that matter.

I was also thinking about Grandpa. He would be trying to get Carl in the telescopic sight, but the Chrysler was between him and Carl. If he got off a shot it would probably have to be at Carl's head if he could see it above the car top. Could Grandpa even tell who had fired the shot?

I was also wondering if Carl would fire again and, if so, would he put another slug into Van Moot or would I be his target? While these thoughts raced through my mind, my right hand was in motion toward the Beretta inside my waistband. I was asking myself where to aim and deciding on a heart shot rather than going for the head because I expected to receive at least one slug before I could fire and my accuracy would likely be affected. I needed the bigger target.

Carl turned his weapon toward me. He saw that he had plenty of time and so very deliberately he brought the pistol to bear on my torso. The window glass on the front of the Chrysler exploded sending a cloud of sparkling fragments between Carl and me, and then the sound of the deer rifle reached our ears. Unable to get a bead on Carl, Grandpa had fired into the front window on the driver's side and the bullet had come out the front window on the passenger's side, narrowly missing Carl. I could see his coat glistening with glass dust and small fragments as he recoiled backward. By the time he recovered I had my own pistol aimed at him.

"Drop it, Carl! That's my backup with a rifle. Make a move and you're dead meat."

He looked puzzled and undecided.

"I mean it, Carl," I shouted at him. "Last chance! Drop the weapon or die."

Carl looked at me and then looked into the darkness where the shot had come from. Reluctantly, he dropped his pistol. Antoinette had stood like a statue until now. She moved to Carl's side and put her arm around his waist. Van Moot was still on his knees, but now he was clutching his abdomen with both hands. I called 911 on my cell and got both an ambulance and a police car on the way.

Grandpa and Ernest Holt came into view at about the same time. Grandpa was approaching carefully with both hands on the rifle, ready to get off another shot if required. He reminded me of the many times I had watched him move up to flush a covey of quail. *Bless his heart!*

Holt had his pistol in his hand as he ran up the driveway. Van Moot was hurting but he was still thinking clearly. "Go get the car and load that device into it," he told Holt.

"Right!" said Holt and started back down the driveway on as fast a run as had brought him.

Holt evidently kept himself in excellent physical shape. He must have run like a Dallas Cowboy fullback to the car because he was back before police or ambulance came. He opened the trunk and heaved Vince's device into it all by himself without breaking a sweat. He slammed the trunk lid down and turned to Van Moot for further instructions.

The night watchman had also called the police. He told us that when he appeared from around the front corner of the building gun in hand. He kept looking back and forth between his immediate supervisor, Carl, and his overall supervisor, me. Neither of us gave him any orders so he just stood there like the rest of us waiting for the cops. Holt tried to get his boss to lie down, but apparently the pain kept him in a bent over position. He was sitting on his heels and rocking back and forward a little. He looked up at Carl and Antoinette. "I'll help you if you help me," he said.

Carl nodded. I understood. They had just agreed that Van Moot would use the tremendous resources of the diamond industry to get them as light a sentence as possible providing he kept his mouth shut about the existence of the diamond-making machine. And that's the way it went down, both here with the police and later at Carl's hearing.

CHAPTER 40
LOOSE ENDS

Holt started to get into the ambulance with his boss, but Van Moot wasn't having that. "Stay with Mr. Kidd," he said. He was a business-first guy if I ever met one.

The two cops politely escorted Carl and Antoinette to the back seat of the police cruiser while Holt joined Grandpa and me in my rental car. Grandpa made a point of getting into the back seat of the maroon Avalon with the rifle and that was fine with me. It was plain to me if not to Ernest that Grandpa was still covering my back—not with the rifle, which would have been awkward in the confines of the car, but with the semi-automatic pistol he was carrying somewhere on his person. If Holt had tried a carjacking, Grandpa would have scattered his brains on the windshield.

Holt was a little reluctant to leave the car when I pulled up at his hotel. "Where's your car, Ernest? I asked.

"Over there." He pointed.

I pulled the Avalon alongside his car. "Well, it's your choice. You can leave the device in my car and it will spend the night in a locked garage watched over by a burglar alarm, or you can load it into your car and leave it unprotected all night in the parking lot."

"I'll load it into my car. But it won't be unprotected because I'll sit up with it."

"That suits me right down to the ground, Ernest. The sooner and the farther I get away from that thing the happier I'll be." And I pulled over to his car, which I suppose was a rental. I popped the trunk and he got out, but I didn't. He had shown already that he could handle the object without help. He accomplished that task quickly while Grandpa changed from the back to the front seat. I waved casually as I drove away. *There, Vince! I hope you're happy.*

It was after three *ante meridian* when Grandpa and I pulled into Vanessa's driveway. She was still up and she opened the door before we got to it.

"Buddy's asleep," she said as she took one of Grandpa's hands with one of hers and one of mine with the other. Her eyes were shining and I thought how great it was to be loved by a woman.

"It's all over," I said.

"Was there any danger?"

"Yeah, Grandpa saved my life. I would have been shot without him."

"Well," Grandpa said, "from the way it worked out I guess it's a good thing I couldn't get a clear shot at him and had to try to get him through the car windows. If his head had shown better over the roof I would have put that bullet right in the middle of it."

"This way is better. For one thing you would have at least been held for questioning and it might have taken a while to clear you."

We went into a little three-way hugging fest before we went into the dining room to give Vanessa the details.

I visited Van Moot late the next morning, really that same morning. He was already out of the Intensive Care Unit and ensconced in a regular room. He was partially propped up with the expected IV tube and electronic monitor wires. I believe I caught a glimpse of an actual, if fleeting, smile when he saw me. I didn't bring flowers.

"How bad is your wound?"

"It was a small caliber pistol, a .22 I think. It perforated the small intestine and lodged in a muscle in the back. They removed it without difficulty and repaired the damage to the intestines. I will be all right provided peritonitis doesn't occur. It shouldn't; they're giving me antibiotics to prevent that. I can't eat for a few days, but should be released within the week."

"I'm willing to go along with your version," I said. "But I would like to know one thing. Was all the crap I've put up with due to Carl? The run-in with thugs on the street, the burglary, and being run off the highway—was that all Carl or did you have a hand in any of that?"

"I think you have been predisposed by the entertainment media to think that the villain is always some big corporation. That's almost a requirement for action movies nowadays. The mysterious evil forces always come from greedy capitalists, either that or some non-existent secret military or CIA adjunct. Thugs for hire are available almost anywhere, even in towns like Tyler, Texas. All Carl would have to do is look for them."

I noticed that he hadn't answered my question, but I let it drop. Van Moot was beginning to look tired, so I left.

When I got to DataDigm after lunch, there was Jack McKinney's secretary sitting in the reception area in Antoinette's place. It turned out that Antoinette never set foot in the building again, not even to pick up personal items.

It was a different story for Carl Hindman. He came into my office a little after three, out on bond already. He looked sad and tired, which I suppose he was, but no more so than any employee might look who had been fired and told to clean out his desk.

"I thought I ought to at least tell you I'm sorry for the trouble I've caused you," he said. "I'm cleaning out my desk, and I'll be out of your life forever when I leave. If you like you can check on the things I'm taking with me just to be sure I'm not stealing something. I just came by to give you this. Please pass it on to Van Moot." And he put one of the large antique-style diamonds in my hand.

"Sit down, Carl. There are a couple of things I'd like to ask you. What puzzles me most is why you shot Van Moot. He was telling you that you were free to leave. All he wanted was Vince's machine."

"Ah, Mike, that's the hell of it. If you had been here in the beginning you could appreciate what I was feeling. Vince wasn't alone in building that device. Several of us helped with different parts. I worked on the original substrate engineering. Vince was a genius; I admit that. He figured out how to keep the diamonds from fluorescing, and he deserved to get rich. But when the money from those contracts came pouring in, there was enough for all of us, all the old-time engineers and programmers, to be rich."

"Vince did give stock to all of you, didn't he? And the profit from those fake contracts benefited all the stockholders."

"Sure, but that was chicken feed compared to what he was making. I don't know how many others figured it out, but when those analysis programs—and they were vastly overpriced—started coming in I put two and two together. Vince was being paid off for his invention."

"Did you talk to Vince about it?"

"No, Vince wouldn't have changed his mind. He never did about anything. He never made a mistake. He was smarter than anybody else and he never let you forget it.

"But every time he got sick and had to leave the business, I made it my policy to work on his device at night, trying to figure it out, reverse engineering it to find the secret. Vince had dismantled it and put it in the junk room to be cannibalized. I moved all the parts into the storage room and reassembled them. By the way, when did you figure out that I was the one giving you trouble?"

"When we couldn't get the door to the supply room opened I figured that's where the device was stashed. As head of security you could open any lock in the building. You could have been working on that thing at night after everyone had gone home. Then it seemed obvious that you were stalling about getting the lock replaced."

"I figured I had to remove it. I made the mistake of not doing it before. You don't know the sacrifices I made. My wife left me because I was never at home. After she left I thought about moving it home. Of course, the storage room at DataDigm had the advantage of providing me with power supplies and other ancillary equipment, but I should have moved it home anyway. That's what I was doing when you stopped me. I'd spent months reconstructing that machine and getting it to operate and here was that Dutchman telling me he was going to take it. I didn't intend to kill him, only stop him long enough for me to get away with that device."

"You were going to shoot me, too."

"Yes, but I still wasn't thinking of killing. All I could think of was that you and Van Moot were standing in my way. I knew once I shot the two of you that I would have to go on the run. A wild idea hit me that Antoinette and I could go into hiding somewhere while I made up enough diamonds to get us set up in Mexico or somewhere. We could still have our dream of vast wealth if we could just get away. I would have had an ideal life with the woman I loved. That's all I was thinking about."

"What did you think you had to gain by setting goons on me?"

"There weren't any goons, just me and one guy. He's not connected to DataDigm and I don't want to name him unless I have to."

"Eugene Willis Carlton," I said. That was the name on the driver's license I took off the big man at the state park.

Carl stared at me. "I guess I've underestimated you all along." Evidently Eugene hadn't reported to him about the licking I gave him.

"Anyway," Carl continued, "I figured that Martin Spencer probably was involved with writing the software for the device. One day he and I were talking about flash drives from the security standpoint. I asked him if one could be programmed so that nobody that didn't have a password could open it. He said that was easy and mentioned that he had programmed one for Vince that would open without a password, but would show how many times it had previously been opened. That's when I figured Vince had put everything on that flash drive and left it with you. All my efforts were strictly to recover that flash drive."

"But you could already make diamonds."

"I could make only one size and pattern, and I had learned that the pattern was rare and distinctive. I needed the software to make other patterns. If I could have gotten that flash drive, I would really have been in business. Oh, well. At first I thought you had it with you. I was having Eugene tail you. When I got word you were headed for Houston, I realized you were going there to retrieve the flash drive. Eugene was driving that truck—his truck—when we forced you off the road. I'm glad you weren't killed. You didn't have the drive on you so I was back to square one."

I thought that over for a few seconds. "Were you the driver when the three goons assaulted Grandpa, Buddy, and me on the sidewalk, or was it Eugene?"

"Now you've got me. I don't know what you're talking about."

"No? At any rate when you shot Van Moot you're lucky he didn't die."

"Yeah, I'd be charged with murder. I'm lucky that Van Moot wanted that device about as badly as I did. He also wants to keep its existence secret. That's why he let me off."

I had several talks with Van Moot in his hospital room. He told me that Carl was going to waive his right to a jury trial and everything would be decided by a judge at a hearing. He laid out the strategy, and I agreed to go along with it.

When the hearing finally came around Carl was represented by a high-priced Dallas lawyer, courtesy of Van Moot. Antoinette testified as a witness; she was never charged with anything. She said she was merely helping a friend move something and had no idea that any theft was involved.

I testified that I had suspected someone of stealing at night and had set up the stake-out. I had asked Van Moot and his assistant to help catch a thief. I told the court that we had caught the pair with the loading door open and hand-truck ready for use—but empty. I was perjuring myself, but it seemed to me then—and still does—that it was the right thing to do. I even said that in my opinion Carl had not intended to fire the shot that hit Van Moot. He was nervously waving the gun around and it went off.

Van Moot took the stand. He seemed a little thinner but otherwise completely recovered from his wound. He gave essentially the same testimony as I did. Carl got a slap on the wrist, a suspended sentence for intent to commit a felony and—this is the part that I liked—a fine for carrying a concealed weapon without a license.

Grandpa's testimony was simply that I had asked him to back me up in case I needed it, which was the truth. As I had urged him, he said that he had fired only a "warning shot" and not that he had tried to hit Carl through the car windows. I think he was glad to do that because he would have been embarrassed to say he missed.

Ernest Holt also testified. His words were almost identical with his boss's. Surprise, surprise! After the hearing I talked with him briefly.

"Your grandpa made a great backup man," he said. "You know, you never told us that all the time you and I and Van Moot were waiting in the grass that old fellow was crouching back there in the bushes with a scope-sighted rifle. Now I wonder whether he was protecting you from Carl Hindman or from me."

"Well, Grandpa is pretty protective and I'm his grandchild. I imagine he was ready to pop off anyone who aimed a weapon at me."

Ernest smiled. "Also, I had the strange feeling when he was riding behind me in your car that he had a pistol in addition to the rifle, and that he had me covered all the way back to the hotel."

"You're right about that, Ernest. And, although it wouldn't have mattered at that range, he's a crackerjack pistol shot."

"I'll bet he is. He's not bad with a walking stick, either." He winked at me as he turned away to join Van Moot.

EPILOGUE

That's about it. Vince's little parting game left me financially better off than when I started, but not as much as you might have expected. I had millions of dollars in synthetic diamonds that were practically indistinguishable from naturals, but cashing them in would bring on the wrath of the diamond cartel.

I felt it would be safe occasionally to sell one of the smaller stones to bring in a few thousand dollars a year. But the real value was in the big stones, and selling one of those would set off an alarm because of their distinctive cut. Maybe by the time I become an old man it will be safe to sell them, assuming that diamonds will still be regarded as precious stones.

I still have considerable stock in DataDigm, but no longer controlling interest. With Vince out of the game Van Moot has no reason to keep renewing the data analysis contracts and so they will peter out. For whatever his reasons, he decided not to cancel any of them so they won't all come to an end at the same time.

Whether the company can survive the loss of those contracts is a moot question, meaning an arguable question not a Van Moot question. I wanted to cash out of all my stock, but both the lawyer Thomas Jackson and Jim Martinez, the company comptroller, won't let me because of government regulations regarding insider trading.

According to them DataDigm's next annual report must disclose the anticipated loss of the mining and drilling data analysis contracts, and this is sure to depress the price of shares. So I sold as much as they thought I could get away with, but that leaves me with much more than I want.

I wanted to get away from the responsibility of managing the company so after selling as much as allowed I gave enough away to bring me well below the fifty percent level. I gave it to Jack McKinney and the other old time employees and set aside a batch of shares to be doled out annually to all the employees. I hope eventually to receive dividends on what I have left, but that is not likely to happen for several years, if ever.

I gave up my fancy office after packing up all the puzzles and scientific toys and bringing them home to Buddy. I expected him to like them, but he didn't take an interest in most of them. He couldn't seem to grasp what the object was. The few he did like he immediately solved and he keeps them and solves them over and over. I have Vince's Monopoly clock hanging in my home office and it reminds me of him every time I glance up at it.

I finally faced up to the fact that I am Mike Kidd and not Vince Talbot. I know now that I was not cut out to run a business, which is why I resigned. Vince was a man of incredible talents. He was an ambitious workaholic who somehow enjoyed playing with work and working at play. They were all the same to him. Life to him was a contest and he was a born competitor. And a born winner.

Carl Hindman divorced his wife and married Antoinette Black. I see them together occasionally. He's now a partner in a tire store. I don't know where he got the capital, but I can't help wondering if he produced a few more diamonds than the two he admitted to. We speak to each other politely but not cordially. Sometimes I fantasize about running him off the road.

My life has returned to almost what it was before, but there are a few changes. I help Grandpa more on his ranch. I've bought a few head of cattle to graze the fields and Grandpa and I work the herd together on shares. I also run a few head on my own small farm.

We've set up a pistol range down by the creek on Grandpa's place where we burned the briefcase and we compete with each other. When he stopped carrying, he set the late model .40 caliber aside and went back to his old army Colt .45. I usually shoot the 9 mm Beretta. Sometimes he beats me and sometimes I beat him. But here's the difference between me and Vince. I enjoy it more when Grandpa beats me.

One thing that has changed about my life is that I no longer have to take an occasional job to supplement my income. The funny thing is that I sort of miss that. I used to enjoy learning a new skill and I used to enjoy quitting when it became routine.

I still take a college course every now and again and I suppose I am the oldest undergraduate at the University of Texas, Tyler, campus. Vanessa thinks I should take the few remaining courses to get a bachelor's degree at least, if not a master's. But I don't know. Studying something I'm interested in is fun. Studying something that bores me is work.

There's no doubt that Vince's briefcase brought about changes. Grandpa changed my life, too. The talk I overheard between him and Vanessa while waking up in the hospital got to me. I think I have finally forgiven my father for deserting his family—well, almost forgiven him.

We all seem to be so much the products of things we have no control over that I begin to wonder if we even have free will. People argue about nature versa nurture. Some seem to think we are molded by our genes while others claim it's all in the way we are raised. It looks to me as if both are involved in about a fifty-fifty proposition, but whatever the relative importance we don't have any choice in the matter.

Maybe we are all like a little boy sitting on a merry-go-round horse. He kicks the horse's flanks and pulls on the reins and yells "Whoa!" and "Giddy-up!" pretending that he's in control. Meanwhile the horse goes through its programmed motions in its predetermined path. At any rate, I have tried to be more tolerant of other people's failings and I feel better for it.

Grandpa gave me another lesson that I've taken to heart. He said I didn't have enough friends. I have tried to fill the void left by Vince's death by reaching out a little more. So my social life has broadened just a little to include a few people that I am at least beginning to feel a fondness for. These include Jim Martinez, who is now running DataDigm and doing a pretty decent job of it. I also stop in and visit Jean Hebert more often and have taken Vanessa with me to visit him and his wife at their home. Two new people I enjoy spending time with are Gar Paine and Martin Spencer.

As he promised, Gar Paine did come through Tyler to pick me up for a fishing trip on Lake Fork. We've gotten to be pretty good friends since then and I sometimes go to Houston to attend his game. With more capital behind me I am doing a little better in a high stakes game, but I spend more time visiting with Gar than playing. I go dove hunting with him on some of his leases. He acquired the leases by allowing some of his rancher players to pay off their debts with hunting rights on their land. I have been at his home several times and each time it seems to be more cluttered and disorganized than it was before.

The last time I was there the phone rang but Gar made no effort to pick up the receiver even though it was right by him on an end table. After several rings it stopped and then Betty yelled out from somewhere, "Herman, it's for you!"

"Goddamn it, Betty, you talk to them. I'm busy."

"You better take this one. It sounds serious."

He picked up the phone. "This is Gar," he said.

He listened in silence for a few seconds and then yelled into the phone, "I hope you do, you son-of-bitch, because when you get here I'm going to kick your ass till your nose bleeds!" Then he slammed the receiver down, turned back to me and continued our conversation about bird hunting in his usual calm voice, "Yeah, the white wing doves are moving farther north every season. I expect we'll get as many of them as mourning doves next week."

Another man I now count as a friend is Martin Spencer, the computer guru. About once a week I pick him up at work and we have lunch together. Every meal includes a lecture from him on food. Last week I learned about the differences between old world and new world spices. That was at a pizza place so I also got a discourse on the history of pizza, how it changed when it immigrated to America, and how it reached its perfection in Chicago-style deep dish. I had suggested that we go to a seafood restaurant but he was in the mood for pizza.

"I'll tell you what," Martin said, "we'll compromise. We'll go to the pizza parlor and have pizza with anchovies."

His sense of humor won me over, so we had pizza—but without anchovies.

Buddy's life has broadened, also. He now has a third home, spending about as much time at Vanessa's house as at our own or Grandpa's. She's taught Buddy to use an electronic digital reader. She downloads books for him by the dozens. Mostly they're free but sometimes she pays for something she thinks he will especially like.

The trouble is he doesn't want to remove anything to make space for new books. So when one reader fills up—and they hold hundreds of titles—she buys him a new one. He now has a bookshelf holding several fully loaded readers. He takes one down in order, reads from it, turns is over and replaces it on the shelf, just the way he does paper books.

Of course, the most important change the briefcase made was bringing Vanessa into my life. I have been thinking of proposing marriage. If I do, I can provide my cousin Jean Hebert with a terrific diamond to mount as an engagement ring. I don't hesitate out of fear of rejection. If she turned me down I would just add that ring to the other in my collection of rejects.

She's great with Buddy and seems to genuinely love him and Grandpa, too. But I have this vague feeling that Vanessa is a little disappointed in me. I think Vince remains her ideal for what a man should be, and he was ambitious. She would have liked to see me grab the bull by the horns and manage DataDigm, partly to keep involved in something created by Vince. She quit her job after learning of her inheritance, saying who would work at a job they didn't like if they didn't have to. Yet she seems to have a different standard for me. I guess a little time will sort this out.